# The Sound of Applause

## Apause

*A Rebecca Classic*
*Volume 1*

*by* Jacqueline Dembar Greene

★ American Girl®

Published by American Girl Publishing
Copyright © 2014 American Girl

Questions or comments? Call 1-800-845-0005,
visit **americangirl.com**, or write to Customer Service,
American Girl, 8400 Fairway Place, Middleton, WI 53562.

Printed in China
15 16 17 18 19 20 LEO 11 10 9 8 7 6 5

This book is a work of fiction. Any similarity to real persons, living or dead,
is coincidental and not intended by American Girl. References to real events,
people, or places are used fictitiously. Other names, characters, places, and
incidents are the products of imagination.

Cover image by Michael Dwornik and Juliana Kolesova

Cataloging-in-Publication Data available from the Library of Congress

*To my mother, Rachel B. Dembar,*
*who opened my world to dolls and books*

*To my great-grandparents, Max and Yetta*
*Webber, who bravely left Dvinsk, Russia,*
*to make a new life in America*

*And to my aunts and uncles, who*
*made every holiday memorable*

# Beforever™

The adventurous characters you'll meet in
the BeForever books will spark your curiosity
about the past, inspire you to find your voice
in the present, and excite you about your future.
You'll make friends with these girls as you share
their fun and their challenges. Like you, they are
bright and brave, imaginative and energetic,
creative and kind. Just as you are, they are
discovering what really matters: Helping others.
Being a true friend. Protecting the earth.
Standing up for what's right. Read their stories,
explore their worlds, join their adventures.
Your friendship with them will BeForever.

# ❦ TABLE *of* CONTENTS ❧

# A Sabbath Surprise

ebecca Rubin tugged at her wooden doll until the top and bottom pulled apart to reveal a smaller doll nesting inside. There were seven painted dolls in all, each one tucked inside the next. They reminded Rebecca of her family, which numbered exactly seven.

The dolls had belonged to Mama when she was back in Russia, before Rebecca was born. But now the Russian dolls were Rebecca's treasure. She lined them up along the parlor windowsill, behind the sheer curtains.

"Ladies and gentlemen, your attention please!" said Rebecca to her imaginary audience. Slowly she drew back the curtains and wiggled the doll she thought of as the mother to the front of the windowsill stage.

"It's almost sundown," Rebecca said in a no-nonsense mama voice. "I hope you've all had your baths." She moved the mama closer to one of the smaller dolls. "Beckie, dear," she said sweetly, "you are so grown-up now. Tonight *you* may light the candles."

Rebecca pretended two of the bigger dolls were her older sisters. She moved them to face the mama and squawked in a high voice, "She's not old enough! She's practically a baby!" The two big sister dolls butted into the little Beckie doll, and it wobbled close to the edge of the windowsill.

Rebecca pushed the papa doll until it stood in front of the others. "Well, curl my mustache," she said in a deep voice. "Beckie's not a baby anymore. She knows the Hebrew blessing perfectly. She is certainly old enough to light the candles tonight."

Before Rebecca could make her brother dolls speak, Mama's very real voice broke into her performance.

"Beckie, you'll have to put away your dolls," she called from the kitchen. "It's time to set the table."

"Phooey!" Rebecca said under her breath. She let the curtains fall across her dolls and turned back to the parlor. Extra leaves had been placed in the table to make room for everyone, and Rebecca smoothed the large white tablecloth. She set out two silver candlesticks and placed one white candle in each.

Every Friday, Mama cooked and cleaned all day to prepare for the Sabbath. Bubbie, Rebecca's grandmother, came down from her apartment upstairs to help cook. Before the sun set, the family came together for a special dinner. Friday night was Rebecca's favorite time of the week. *But Mama should let me do something more important than just setting the table*, she thought as she lifted a tall stack of Mama's best dishes from the sideboard.

Mama looked in from the kitchen. "Don't carry too many plates at once!" she cautioned. "And we need one extra tonight."

"Who's coming?" Rebecca asked, adding a plate and dividing the pile in two. Through the doorway, she could see Bubbie frying fish in a black iron pan. Mama and Bubbie glanced at each other, without answering her question.

That made Rebecca even more curious to know who would be sharing their Sabbath dinner. "Who is it, Mama?"

Mama stirred sizzling potatoes and onions as she answered. "My cousin, Moyshe."

Now Rebecca nearly did drop the plates. "The

actor?" she asked. She had overheard her parents talking about Moyshe before, but she had never met him. He usually traveled around the country, acting in vaudeville shows, but other times he was out of work and needed to borrow money from Papa. Rebecca had always wondered what an actor was like in real life, when he wasn't onstage. Tonight she would find out.

Rebecca took special care setting the table. She folded the linen napkins so that the crocheted edges were lined up neatly. If a real actor was coming to dinner, she wanted everything to be perfect.

"Sadie! Sophie!" Bubbie called. A few strands of gray hair slipped from her neat bun and framed her round face. She opened the oven door and slid out two braided loaves of *hallah* bread. Bubbie only baked hallah for Friday nights and holidays. Each loaf needed two eggs, and eggs were expensive.

Rebecca's twin sisters hurried in, wearing matching dresses. Sadie's eyes sparkled, and she looked eager to help. Sophie followed behind her.

"Come check if hallah is done," Bubbie instructed them.

"But the loaves are so hot," Sophie complained. She

pulled away from the open oven. Sadie wasn't timid at all. She rapped two fingers against the shiny crust. A hollow sound echoed back.

"Done," Sadie announced.

*Why doesn't Bubbie ever ask me to check the bread?* Rebecca wondered. *Bubbie treats me like a little child!* She pushed past her sisters.

"I can do it, too," she said.

"So, give a tap," Bubbie told her. "When dough is done, bread sounds empty."

As Rebecca knocked on the bread with her knuckles, her older brother, Victor, sneaked up and rapped on her head. "Done!" he teased. The twins giggled.

Rebecca tried to swat Victor's arm, but before she could catch him, a rhythmic knock sounded at the kitchen door. Everyone turned to stare as it creaked open. A tall young man wearing a jaunty straw hat and holding a polished cane poked his head into the room.

"Moyshe!" Mama exclaimed.

The man put his finger to his lips, signaling everyone to be quiet, and began sprinkling something in the doorway. Rebecca couldn't see anything in his hand.

Her little brother, Benny, squatted down. He looked at the floor, and then up at Moyshe.

"What you are putting on this clean floor?" Bubbie cried.

Moyshe peered into the hallway and looked around nervously. Then he made more frantic sprinkling motions. Finally, he spoke. "It's lion powder," he said solemnly.

Rebecca frowned. "What in the world is that?"

"Why, don't you know?" Moyshe asked. "It keeps the lions away."

Benny's eyes grew wide. "Lions?"

Sadie sniffed. "That's ridiculous. There aren't any lions around here."

"You see how well it works!" Moyshe announced.

Benny heaved a sigh of relief. Sadie and Sophie shook their heads at the silly joke. Rebecca burst out laughing.

Moyshe flashed a gleaming smile. "At least one person in this audience likes my joke," he said. "If you make them laugh, your audience will love you." He winked at Rebecca. "Remember that!"

Rebecca had never imagined that Mama's cousin

would be so exciting. He even looked interesting, with his bright dark eyes and the cane draped over his arm.

"Come in and close the door, Moyshe," Mama said.

"Excuse me, but it's no more Moyshe Shereshevsky," her cousin said. "I am Max Shepard, if you please." He gave a low bow, sweeping his hat off his head. "An American name for an American actor."

"America," Bubbie grumbled. "Always changing with the names. You don't change a name like a dirty shirt!"

Max didn't argue. "You must be little Beckie," he said, giving Rebecca his full attention. "You were toddling around like a windup doll the last time I saw you. Now you're a young lady!"

Rebecca beamed. Visitors never talked to her first when they met the family—they always fussed over Sadie and Sophie because they thought twins were so remarkable. If only they knew how left out Rebecca felt, being their younger sister!

Max turned to Benny. "And you weren't even born! Now you're old enough to grow buttons."

"Buttons don't grow!" Benny said.

Max pulled something from Benny's ear. "This

sure looks like a button to me."

Benny's eyes grew wide as Max dropped a shiny brown button into his hand. Rebecca chuckled. How did Max do it?

"And this must be the *Bar Mitzvah* boy!" Max exclaimed, shaking Victor's hand. "Your mother tells me you're almost thirteen now, and studying hard for your Bar Mitzvah." He dropped his voice lower, as if sharing a secret. "But I hear sneaking out to play baseball is a lot more fun than studying Hebrew." Victor grinned.

"Good *Shabbos!*" Rebecca's grandfather called as he and Papa came in. Grandpa and Bubbie often mixed Yiddish words with their English. Yiddish was the language most Jewish immigrants in the neighborhood spoke. Rebecca could speak it, too, and she knew Shabbos meant Sabbath.

Papa handed Mama a penny bouquet of flowers, as he did every Friday. "Almost as pretty as you," he smiled. Mama blushed at the compliment as she hung her apron on a nail by the stove.

"Good evening, Moyshe," Papa said, shaking hands.

"Excuse me, but that's Max," Bubbie corrected him. "There is no more Moyshe."

Max grinned. "Moyshe, Max, what's the difference? You can call me anything, as long as you don't call me late for dinner!"

Rebecca thought Max was funny. He was nothing like Papa, who was usually so serious.

"Such a busy day at the shoe store," Grandpa said. "But now it's Shabbos, and time to rest."

Papa took the *pushke*, the tin charity box, from the kitchen shelf. Every Friday night he put in his loose change. When the box was full, Papa brought the money to the synagogue. The congregation used the funds they collected to help new immigrants. Papa dropped in the coins from his pocket, and they clanged to the bottom.

Grandpa added some change. "We must always help those who are less fortunate," he said. He held the box out to Max, but just at that moment Max stepped into the parlor and started tickling Benny until he was screaming with laughter.

"Don't make him wild," Mama scolded. "Come, it's time to light the candles."

Benny dashed to Papa and pulled at his sleeve. "My turn! My turn!"

Papa lifted Benny in the air, and he squealed with delight. "Women light the Shabbos candles," Papa said.

"No fair!" Benny whined.

"Can't I light them tonight?" Rebecca begged. "I know the prayer by heart."

"You heard Papa," Sadie said. "It's for the *women* in the family."

Rebecca frowned. This was just like her windowsill play!

"The twins will light the candles," Mama said firmly. "After all, they're fourteen."

"And not married yet?" Max joked. "Time to call the matchmaker!" The twins put their hands over their mouths and tried to stifle their giggles.

Rebecca went to the windowsill and poked the big sister dolls so hard, they rocked a little. "When will *I* get to light the candles?" she muttered. "The twins get to do *everything!*"

"Stop pouting and help," Bubbie ordered. She set a soup tureen on the sideboard and ladled golden chicken soup into bowls. Rebecca served Max first. He closed his eyes and breathed deeply, as if smelling a sweet perfume.

The family waited while Bubbie hung her apron in the kitchen. Then she sat down and straightened the lacquer pin she often wore. It was a keepsake she had brought with her from Russia. Rebecca had always loved the picture of the leaping hare that was painted on the pin's shiny black background. The picture was from a Russian folktale called Clever Karina.

Sadie and Sophie stood before the silver candlesticks. Everyone watched as they lit the white candles with a long wooden match. Then they closed their eyes and recited the Hebrew prayer together, giving thanks for the Sabbath, a day of rest and peace. The candles flickered, lighting up the twins' faces with a golden glow.

"Beautiful," Max murmured. The grown-ups nodded approvingly, and Rebecca felt a bubble of envy grow in her chest. She was old enough to do more than just set the table!

Victor raised the special cup of Sabbath wine and recited the Hebrew blessing. Grandpa corrected his pronunciation, and Rebecca felt secretly pleased. Next, Mama removed the delicately embroidered hallah cover from the warm bread. She held up the two loaves, and the whole family gave thanks for their food.

Rebecca said the prayer loudly so that everyone would know *she* didn't make mistakes.

Rebecca sipped her steaming soup, with Mama's homemade noodles. She loved the foods that made Friday nights special. But tonight she wasn't think-ing about dinner. An idea was flickering in her mind, forming a glow as bright as the Sabbath candles.

# A Showy Dinner

ama set platters of food on the table, and Max spooned out a big helping of pota- toes. "There's a new play coming to the Yiddish theater," he announced.

"Such a long time it's been since we see a play!" Grandpa said.

"We don't want to see Yiddish plays," Sadie said. "We like moving pictures." As usual, Sophie didn't say a word, but she nodded in agreement.

"Moving pitch-es," Grandpa said in his thick accent. "Why you want to see people moving in pitch-es, when you can see real people moving onstage?"

"Movies are smooth," Sophie said. "We're going to see a show tomorrow with our friends."

Grandpa seemed puzzled. "What is this *smooth*?"

"It means modern and exciting!" said Sadie.

Rebecca could only imagine what a moving picture looked like. She had seen posters advertising the newest movies, but she had never been to one. "Can I come?" she asked.

The twins stopped their spoons in midair. With one voice they replied, "You're not old enough."

"You always leave me out," Rebecca argued.

"We're in high school," Sadie reminded her, as if Rebecca hadn't heard that a thousand times.

"There's plenty of time for that nonsense when you're older," Papa declared. "I don't think these new movie pictures are meant for children."

Rebecca fumed. The twins got to do everything together. Even at night, they whispered under their covers while her bed stood alone on the opposite side of the room.

Victor glanced at Grandpa with an impish grin and then turned to Benny. "Speaking of pitch-es," he said to his brother, "how about catching baseballs for me tomorrow afternoon?"

Benny wiggled with excitement. "I can get the ball even if it rolls under the fence!"

*The twins are best friends, and Victor and Benny can*

*play ball together,* Rebecca thought, *but I have only myself.
I'm always left out, even on Friday nights.*

Rebecca thought of her friend Rose. She had her own
candlesticks and lit the candles beside her mother every
Sabbath. *If I had some candlesticks of my own,* Rebecca
thought, *Mama would have to let me light candles.* Her
idea began to glow more brightly. She could stand right
next to Sadie and Sophie. Then they'd see she was old
enough to perform the ceremony, and even old enough
to go to the movies!

"I heard the Boston Red Sox have a new player,"
Max said, taking two crispy pieces of fish. "His name's
Babe Ruth."

"Babe?" Bubbie scowled. "This is a name?"

"I read about him in the paper," Victor said importantly. "They say he's going to be an ace pitcher. I wish
he was playing for the Yankees."

"If he's good," Max said, "maybe we'll sign him
next year."

"Enough about baseball," Papa said. "Now that
school has started, I want to hear how my children
are doing."

"In English class, we're reading a wonderful play

called *Hamlet*," Sadie announced.

"It's by William Shakespeare," Sophie added softly.

Max looked pleased. "Ahh—the very best of theater."

Rebecca butted in. Why should her sisters get all the attention? "I got one hundred and ten percent on my arithmetic test," she announced, looking directly at Papa. "Miss Maloney gave us an extra credit problem, and I even got that right."

"Doing well in school is indeed something to be proud of," Mama said gently, "but be careful not to boast." She wagged her finger at the children. "You don't realize how lucky you are. In Russia, we never had the chance to go to school."

Max nodded in agreement. "Life was hard growing up in Russia. But I have fond memories, too." He lightly touched Bubbie's pin with the picture of the leaping hare. "I remember my mother telling me the story of Clever Karina."

Rebecca knew the story well, as Mama had often told it at bedtime. Max began telling the tale, his deep voice as silky as a singer crooning a tune.

"One morning, a poor farmer was overjoyed to see his horse had given birth to a foal. It was sleeping under a hay wagon in his neighbor's field. His wealthy neighbor said, 'Everyone knows a newborn rests beneath its mother. Since my hay wagon is obviously the mother, that handsome foal is mine.'"

"That's a-diculous!" Benny declared, and everyone chuckled.

Max went on, telling how the poor man told his only child, Karina, what had happened. Rebecca was drawn into the story. She imagined she was little Karina, trying to help. Acting the role, she said in a sweet voice, "Go to the tsar, Father, and ask him to settle the matter."

Max gave Rebecca a broad smile. He reached for Mama's flowered shawl and draped it around Rebecca's head. Now she truly felt as if she was in a play, acting the role of Karina.

Max continued. "But when the tsar heard the story, he did not make a decision. Instead he posed a riddle. The tsar said to the two men, 'You must each bring your youngest daughter to me, but she must not come on foot nor on horseback. She must not wear clothes, but she must not be naked. She must not bring a present, but she must come with a gift. The one who solves my riddle will keep the foal.'"

"Phooey on the tsar!" Grandpa scoffed.

"The poor farmer trudged home," said Max, "and told his daughter of the impossible riddle. But Clever Karina knew just what to do."

Rebecca acted out Karina's solution as Max told the end of the tale. "So Karina wrapped herself in her father's fishnet and rode off to the tsar's palace on the back of a giant hare. In her hand she carried a partridge in a cage. When she arrived before the tsar, Karina held up the birdcage."

Rebecca lifted her hand, looking determined. "Here is a gift, Your Majesty," she said, and she pretended to open a latch on a cage. Her hands made a graceful flapping motion, as if a bird were flying away.

"The tsar was pleased with Karina's clever solution to his riddle and decreed that her father should keep the foal. When Karina grew up, the tsar married her, for he knew he could never find another wife who was nearly as clever."

Max took Rebecca's hand, and she bowed with him as the family clapped. "What an actress!" Max exclaimed. "Our Beckie's a natural talent."

Rebecca could barely breathe. Max thought she was

a good actress—and her whole family was clapping for her!

"I'm auditioning for a movie studio this week," Max said. "Maybe I should bring Beckie along!"

Bubbie rolled her eyes. "Don't give her crazy ideas," she said.

Grandpa slapped the table. "Acting is a no-good life for a young lady!"

"Beckie should be a teacher," Papa said, sitting back comfortably. He seemed quite pleased with this idea.

Rebecca's shoulders slumped. Why didn't Papa think she should become an actress? After all, Max said she had talent.

Papa turned to Victor, ending the discussion. "How about working in the store tomorrow?" he asked.

"Tomorrow he comes with me to synagogue," Grandpa declared. He turned to Victor and said sternly, "So close to your Bar Mitzvah, your Hebrew is not so good!"

Bubbie shook her head at Papa. "Working on Shabbos," she sighed. "Such a shame."

Rebecca knew Jews weren't supposed to work on Saturday, the day of rest. Grandpa worked at the store all week, but on Saturdays he prayed at the synagogue and often took Victor with him.

"I don't like to work on Shabbos, but most people shop on Saturday. I have to keep the store open if it's going to support the family," Papa said.

*Maybe I can't light the candles or go to a movie,* Rebecca thought, *but I can help in Papa's store. Then he'll see how grown-up I am.* If she did a good job, maybe Papa would give her a few pennies. That would help her save for candlesticks.

"I'll work tomorrow," she offered.

"I do need help," Papa said. He stroked his mustache thoughtfully. "Why don't we try it?" Rebecca brightened. "Wear your best shoes," he added.

Max sipped his glass of tea. "What do you hear from your brother Jacob in Russia?" he asked Papa. "Now that Russia is fighting against Germany, they are drafting more men. You know the Russian army takes Jewish boys as young as twelve," Max added. "Jacob's family better get out before the war gets worse."

Lines of worry creased Papa's forehead. "Things are not good," he sighed. He took a letter from his pocket.

"This came from Jacob today." He read the letter, changing it into English.

"Dear Brother, I write to tell you that life here is becoming more dangerous as the war spreads. Jews are no longer allowed to work, and I have lost my job. I am afraid to let Josef and Michael out of the house for fear soldiers will snatch them off the street and force them into the tsar's army. Food is scarce, and we are thankful when we have a bit of cabbage soup. Little Ana is sick and weak from hunger, and I fear she will not survive another winter here. A friend will try to smuggle us out of Russia, but it will take every *kopek* we have left. We beg you to send us ship tickets as soon as possible, so we can join you in New York. Our hearts are filled with sorrow, knowing the hardship this expense will cause, but we cannot wait any longer."

Victor's eyes had a faraway look, and Rebecca wondered if he was imagining what his life would be like if he were in the Russian army. She was glad Victor didn't have to worry about that. Grandpa had said that Jewish boys were often treated harshly and given the most dangerous army jobs. Many boys never saw their families again.

"It's no good in the Old Country," Grandpa said. "From now on, we fill the pushke for family."

Max cleared his throat and looked embarrassed. "I wish I could help," he said, "but I can barely pay for the room I'm renting. Somehow, you've got to send them tickets right away."

"I know," Papa said irritably. "We've been trying to save enough for a long time."

Sophie looked up. "You don't have to give us our allowance every week," she offered.

Rebecca couldn't imagine what it was like not to have enough food to eat. She looked at the dishes on the table. They were empty only because her family had eaten as much as they wanted. Rebecca felt ashamed. She couldn't spend money on candlesticks when her cousin was starving.

"I have a little bit saved, Papa," she said. "Maybe that will help buy the tickets."

Papa shook his head. "Don't worry, children. We need much more than your pennies. I'll find a way to raise the money."

## A Showy Dinner

In bed that night, Sadie and Sophie talked until they fell asleep, but Rebecca lay awake thinking about her cousin. Ana must be so frightened. What if she became too sick to escape? The journey from Russia would be long and dangerous. If only Uncle Jacob's family could make it to New York, Rebecca thought, Ana could be like a sister to her. Ana was exactly her age. Why, it would be just like having a twin.

Rebecca could hear Mama and Papa talking softly in the kitchen. "The ship tickets cost at least thirty dollars each, and we need to buy five of them. All our savings won't be enough," Papa said. "And Jacob must have twenty-five dollars in his pocket to get into America." There was a long silence. Rebecca added up the numbers in her head. Papa needed one hundred seventy-five dollars! How would he ever do it?

Rebecca crept out of bed and opened her trunk. She took out the knotted handkerchief that held her savings and quietly counted. All she had was twenty-seven cents. Maybe she should give all the money to Papa. But it wasn't nearly enough to buy even one ship ticket. And Papa had said he didn't want her savings.

Her wooden dolls lay strewn about in the trunk

where she had tossed them after dinner. She put them back together, each doll nestled safely inside the next, but she held Beckie close as she snuggled under the covers.

"Am I being selfish to want candlesticks for myself?" Rebecca whispered to her doll. In the dim light from the kitchen, she could barely see Beckie's painted smile before she fell asleep.

# One for the Money

### ᕥᕦ CHAPTER 3 ᕤᕥ

ebecca studied the picture on the cover of her sisters' movie magazine. Then she looked again at her own reflection in the mirror that hung in the parlor. She tilted the brim of her hat until it slanted across her forehead. That was just how the movie star Pearl White wore her hat. Rebecca turned her face to one side and then the other, admiring the look. She imagined she was on a movie poster. "Coming Soon! Rebecca Rubin in *The Perils of Pauline!*"

"Stop primping," Mama called. "You'll make Papa late."

"I'm coming!" Rebecca smoothed her cotton stockings and straightened the white collar and cuffs on her dress. Mama always called it her "purple" dress, but Rebecca preferred the elegant description from the mail-order catalog: "Rich violet tweed," it read, "for the sophisticated young lady." Rebecca spit on her finger and rubbed the toes of her matching leather shoes to a shine.

Mama held out the leftover hallah from last night. "Take this up to Bubbie," she said. "Grandpa can have it with his lunch."

"But I'm late," Rebecca complained, running up the stairs two at a time. Through the window on the landing, she glimpsed empty clotheslines strung from the fire escapes. Her Jewish neighbors didn't wash clothes on Saturday. That would be work!

Rebecca opened Bubbie's door and set the bread on the shiny oilcloth that covered the small kitchen table. Sadie and Sophie were in the parlor arguing about how many embroidered napkins they had to make for their wedding chests.

"Napkins, doilies, pillowcases, aprons, tablecloths," Bubbie began, counting on her fingers. "If you don't make them now, you won't have enough linens ready when you start your own home."

"Nobody makes a trousseau anymore, Bubbie," Sadie grumbled. "It's 1914 already, and in America you don't need a trunkful of handmade linens to get married!"

Bubbie came into the kitchen holding the calico bag Rebecca used for her crocheting. "You left your needle-work here," she said.

Rebecca tucked the bag under her arm. "Maybe if it gets slow in the shoe store, I'll make another doily."

Bubbie frowned. "I don't think you should crochet on Shabbos—even crocheting is work."

"I'm already helping in the store," Rebecca reasoned.

Bubbie sighed. "I suppose it couldn't be worse," she admitted.

"You'd better take the pattern book," Sadie said. "You'll need the directions."

"I know them by heart," Rebecca said, turning to go.

Bubbie pinched her cheek. "Such a talent with the crochet hook!" She called to the twins, "Your younger sister makes more than both of you for her wedding chest."

"Bully for her," Sadie scoffed.

Rebecca raced down the steps and out the front door. *If I'm old enough to prepare for my wedding*, she thought, *why aren't I old enough to go to the movies or light the candles?*

Papa stood on the sidewalk, tapping his foot. Rebecca

had wanted the day to be perfect, and already she had spoiled things by being late!

"Sorry, Papa," she began, "I had to fix my hat, and then—"

"My, how dramatic!" Papa smiled, looking at the tilted brim. "So, today you'll be my stylish helper." He put his arm around her shoulder as they walked down East Seventh Street. Papa kept a quick pace, and Rebecca hurried to keep up.

"We'll save a little money and skip the trolley," he said. "But we won't save time. It's a long walk."

If Papa didn't want Rebecca's savings, why did he need to save the five-cent fare for the trolley? She tried not to think about the money they needed for cousin Ana and her family. Rebecca had saved so little—how could she make a difference?

Marigolds bloomed in the window boxes on the row houses in Rebecca's neighborhood. As she and Papa walked, the streets became narrower, and storefronts looked out from the ground floor of tenement buildings. They crossed the busy thoroughfare of East Houston Street, and Rebecca admired the elegant window displays in the shops. At last they turned onto

Rivington Street. Instead of the usual weekday bustle, just a few pushcarts lined the road. Pungent smells of pickles and cheese and herring filled the air. Neighbors passed each other on the street, and Rebecca heard greetings in many different languages.

When she saw the familiar blue awning of Papa's shoe store, she dashed across the street. Papa caught up to her, out of breath.

"Slow down! You have to watch for wagons, and now there are automobiles, too. Those reckless drivers don't look out for little girls."

Rebecca just grinned and reached for the key in Papa's hand. "Let me do it!" She unlocked the front door and the bell on top jingled cheerily, as if to welcome her. She stepped inside and hung a sign in the window. It said OPEN in English, Yiddish, and Italian. Rebecca hung her hat and shawl in the back room and put her calico bag next to a row of shoe boxes.

"I'll start dusting," she offered, taking the feather duster from its hook. She wanted Papa to see that she could be a big help.

Rebecca breathed in the thick, buttery smell of new leather. She loved the way the shoes sat at attention on the narrow shelves as if they were waiting for the chance to march outside. She whisked the dust from the shoes on display, singing as she worked.

"Take me out to the ball game," she sang. "Take me out with the crowd . . ." In the children's area, she brushed lightly over tiny high-topped boots, thick-soled play shoes, and dainty dress shoes with straps that buttoned across the ankle. "Buy me some peanuts and Cracker Jack, I don't care if I never get back!" She dusted women's shoes with pointy toes, fancy buckles, and squashed heels.

"If the ball game is over," Papa joked, "the sidewalk needs sweeping." He handed Rebecca a tattered broom. "The pushcart peddlers leave such a mess Friday after-noon. I have to sweep up so the store looks better. Put on my workshop apron so your dress won't get dirty."

Rebecca wrinkled her nose. She didn't want to put the stained canvas apron over her beautiful dress. Then Papa handed her a pair of worn leather boots. "Wear these instead of your good shoes," he told her. Rebecca started to argue, but she didn't want to annoy Papa. She tied on the big apron and replaced her shiny shoes with the old boots.

Outside, Rebecca consoled herself by pretending she was auditioning for the movie studio with Max. She imagined she was playing a poor immigrant who had to sweep the streets to help her family survive. She pushed the broom slowly to show how exhausted she was. She swept up banana peels, soggy potatoes, and pieces of newspaper blowing against the curb. *Life in America is so hard*, she pretended. *I can't go to school but must work every day for pennies!* She hummed a sad Yiddish song.

Lost in her playacting, Rebecca was startled by Leo Berg, a pesky boy from her class at school. His mother walked beside him. An elegant fur scarf was draped around her neck, ending in a fox's head, tail, and paws that dangled from her shoulders. Mrs. Berg swished inside the shoe store without a glance, but Leo stared at Rebecca while she swept.

"This is my father's store," Rebecca said proudly. "I'm helping today."

"Why, you're nothing but a street sweeper," Leo sniffed, brushing at his jacket.

*Imagining* she was a poor sweeper in a movie was fine, Rebecca thought, but having someone call her one was unbearable! Her face burned with anger.

"Sweeping the sidewalk is very important," she declared. "Maybe if you knew how to work hard, you wouldn't have to wear the dunce cap in school."

Leo's cheeks turned red. "You'd better be polite, or my mother and I will leave!" He stepped inside, slamming the door so hard that the glass pane rattled.

How could she keep quiet when Leo had insulted her? Yet Rebecca couldn't let Papa lose a customer. She swept harder and faster, pushing her anger around with the dirt.

When she finished, she walked straight to the back room and put on her own shoes. As she hung up Papa's apron, she could hear Leo complaining. Rebecca peeked through the curtains that screened off the back room.

"These shoes are ugly!" Leo grumbled.

"We've been to every shoe store on Broadway," Mrs. Berg said. "Leopold didn't like anything!"

Papa sat on a low stool, helping Leo take off a pair of shoes. Open boxes and loose shoes were strewn around the floor. Instead of looking cross, Papa just smiled. "I might have to show you a special pair I've been saving." He hesitated. "I don't know if I should.

These shoes aren't for any ordinary boy."

"*I'm* not an ordinary boy," Leo piped up. "What's so special about them?"

Papa rubbed his chin. "Well," he began, "these shoes are made of the same leather used for cowboy boots."

"I want to try them!" Leo demanded. "I see cowboy boots in Western movies every week."

Rebecca fumed. Leo was her age, and he saw movies every week!

"Oh, do show us the cowboy shoes, Mr. Rubin," Leo's mother said. "I'm at my wit's end! If Leopold likes them, I don't care what they cost."

Papa came into the storage room and searched the boxes stacked according to style and size.

"Cowboy boot leather?" Rebecca whispered.

Papa winked. "Boots or shoes, leather is leather," he said.

Rebecca took her bag of crocheting and walked past Leo without glancing in his direction. Sitting near the bright front window, she looped the thick cotton thread around her crochet hook and pulled the stitches through until a lacy flower design took shape.

Mrs. Berg walked around, inspecting the latest women's shoes. "My, my," she clucked. "Aren't you the clever girl! I didn't know anyone still learned to crochet now that so few young ladies make a trousseau." She picked up a satiny shoe with silk bows.

Rebecca wondered if Sadie and Sophie were right. Maybe girls didn't make linens for their wedding chests anymore. She held her doily higher so that Mrs. Berg could admire it. "Well, I'm only nine and I'm not planning to get married for a long time," Rebecca explained. "But I learned to crochet when I was six, and Bubbie says I have a knack for it."

"That's enough, Rebecca," said Papa. "Let Mrs. Berg browse in peace."

Rebecca pursed her lips. Once again, she had talked too much. If Papa found out what she had said to Leo about the dunce cap, he might send her home!

Mrs. Berg peered closely at the doily. "You couldn't buy such a fine piece for love or money."

Rebecca swelled with pride. Leo's mother was a lot nicer than Leo was. Feeling generous, she took a finished doily from her bag and handed it to Mrs. Berg. "Please take this one," she offered. "I've made so many."

Mrs. Berg patted Rebecca on the head. "What a sweet child." She folded the doily into her purse. "I will certainly enjoy displaying it in our new home. We're moving uptown in the spring, you know."

With a dramatic rustle of tissue paper, Papa unwrapped the shoes. He sniffed the leather. "Ah, the aroma of saddles and boots," he said.

Rebecca fought back a giggle. Why, Papa was an actor, too!

Leo grabbed one of the shoes and smelled it.

"All right," Papa said, "try them. But they might not fit." He eased Leo's foot into the shoe with a shiny brass shoehorn.

"They're perfect for me," Leo announced. He put on the second shoe and laced it up himself. Then he tucked his thumbs into the waist of his knickers and strutted around the room with his chest out.

"Doesn't he look handsome in those shoes!" gushed Mrs. Berg. "He'll wear them home."

"Shall I wrap up the old ones?" Papa asked.

"No," Leo said. "Get rid of them."

Papa went to the cash register, and Rebecca began replacing all the shoes in their proper boxes. She hoped

Papa would notice how neat everything was.

As Mrs. Berg swept toward the door, she bent down and handed Rebecca something. The bell on the door jingled them out, and Rebecca saw a shiny quarter in her hand. Mrs. Berg had paid her for the doily! She didn't want Papa to see. He might tell her to return the money. Her heart thumped as she hid the quarter in her bag and picked up Leo's old shoes.

"What shall I do with these, Papa? They're hardly scuffed."

"They will be put to good use," Papa said. "Set them on the workbench."

Rebecca carried a stack of shoe boxes into the back, along with Leo's old shoes. As she placed his shoes on the workbench, she saw several other pairs of worn children's shoes lined up near cans of shoe polish. The bench was littered with tools, tiny nails, and scraps of leather.

"What will you do with these old shoes, Papa?" she asked.

*Jing-jing!* The bell on the door announced a customer before he could answer. A thin woman with dark braids pinned up around her head stepped inside. A small boy held her hand.

"May I help you?" Papa asked.

"My son's shoes, they are too small," she said in a heavy Italian accent. "A friend says to me you have shoes not cost too much?"

"Sit down," Papa smiled. The boy was about the same age as Benny. He had on a pair of worn knickers, and his stockings were mended around the knees. Papa pushed his thumb against the toe of the boy's shoe. "Definitely a bit snug." He took off the old shoes, and Rebecca saw that the soles were worn all the way through. Papa measured the boy's feet with a wooden measuring slide.

"You'd think my little Joey would have plenty shoes," the woman said, "since his father works in shoe factory."

Papa nodded. "I worked in a shoe factory when I first came here from Russia, and I never had a decent pair of my own. I had to put cardboard in my shoes so my socks wouldn't rub the sidewalk!" Papa picked up the boy's old shoes and said, "Let me see what I can do with these."

Rebecca counted out her stitches, her crochet hook

darting in and out. When the boy looked over his shoulder at her, she winked. He giggled and hid his head in his mother's skirt.

Papa returned holding a polished pair of shoes. "I've fixed them up so they hardly look like the same pair." He slipped the boy's feet into the shoes.

"Look, I can wiggle my toes," Joey exclaimed. He skipped around the store.

Rebecca squinted at the shoes as Joey went by. "They certainly *don't* look like the same pair," she remarked, but Papa's stern look silenced her. Why wasn't she supposed to say what was plain as day? She lowered her eyes and moved only her fingers instead of her mouth.

"How much I owe you?" the woman asked.

"Not a penny," Papa said. "I just fixed his shoes up a bit."

"I thank you so much," the woman said with a grateful smile.

Papa patted the boy's shoulder. "Wear them in good health, Joey." Rebecca watched Joey set off down the street, hopping over cracks in the sidewalk.

"Now you know why I save the old shoes," Papa said quietly. "I keep them for situations just like this."

"Does the lady know what you did?" Rebecca asked.

Papa nodded. "She knows. But it's best not to talk about it, Beckie. No one likes to take charity."

"That was a good thing to do, Papa," said Rebecca. She gave him a hug.

"It's a *mitzvah*," Papa explained. "We should help others whenever we can. Your heart tells you the right thing to do. But you already know that, don't you?"

Rebecca felt a twinge in her own heart as she remembered Ana. Shouldn't she be doing something to help her cousin?

The store grew busier, and thoughts of Ana soon disappeared. As Rebecca carried boxes back and forth, she remembered the quarter in her bag. What if she brought more doilies to the store next week? Maybe Mrs. Berg would come back.

"Papa, could I work with you every Saturday?" she asked.

"We'll see," Papa said. "We'll see."

# Two for the Show

n Sunday afternoon, Rebecca stood at the kitchen sink, trying to clean melted wax from the candlesticks. *Why should I have to clean these,* she thought grumpily, *when I can't even light the candles?*

She scraped at the wax with her fingernail, wondering how much more money she would need to buy her own candlesticks. With the quarter from Mrs. Berg, she had saved just fifty-two cents. Even if she bargained with the peddlers, that wouldn't be enough. Candlesticks would cost at least two dollars.

She thought again of Ana, and her stomach fluttered. Lighting candles wasn't as important as having enough food to eat. Should she give her savings to Papa for the ship tickets? But Papa had already refused her money and told her not to worry.

He would get the tickets soon, wouldn't he?

"'To be, or not to be: that is the question,'" floated a voice from the girls' bedroom. Sadie and Sophie were reading *Hamlet* aloud to each other.

*To buy, or not to buy,* Rebecca thought. *That is* my *question!*

"Vroom! Rrroom!" Benny ran around the parlor holding a toy airplane aloft.

"*Shah!*" Papa hushed him. "Your sisters are studying." He turned the page of his newspaper.

Rebecca walked into the parlor as she polished the gleaming candlesticks with a clean cloth. Through the open window, she could see people strolling along the sidewalks in the mild September air. Neighbors sat on their front stoops, talking and laughing. Victor was off playing stickball, and Mama had gone out. Rebecca didn't want to stay inside tiptoeing around.

She could hear Sadie and Sophie reading Shakespeare's lines with great feeling. But they didn't have an audience, as she'd had when she acted out the folktale with Max. Thinking about performing gave Rebecca an idea. People paid money to see a show! Sometimes children tap-danced right on Orchard

Street, between the peddlers' carts, and shoppers tossed pennies to them.

Rebecca took Mama's summer straw hat from its hook and put it on. Its wide, floppy brim and big pink flowers would get people's attention. She rolled up a black wool scarf and draped it around her neck like Mrs. Berg's fur.

"I'm going out," she called to Papa from the kitchen. She hoped he wouldn't look up from his paper. Rebecca hurried to the door, but she wasn't quick enough.

"Me, too!" Benny demanded, landing his plane on one of Mama's geraniums.

"Take him with you," Papa ordered, "so the twins can study."

Rebecca's heart sank. Taking Benny would ruin her plan. But her brother happily pulled his bag of marbles from a box on the kitchen floor. He grabbed his cap and ran down the steps.

The front stoop of their row house was empty. The carved lions' heads on each side of the door looked down with a silent roar. Rebecca saw the sidewalk below her. *Why, the stoop is just like a stage,* she thought.

"I'm going to put on a show," she said to her brother.

"So just stay out of the way."

"I want to be in a show, too," Benny said.

Rebecca thought for a moment. If she didn't let Benny help out, he would just keep bothering her. "Tell you what—you can play the organ grinder's monkey," she told him. "You go into the crowd and pass your hat around to collect pennies."

Benny started screeching like a monkey and hopping from one foot to the other.

"This is fun!" he cried. "But where's the crowd?"

"We haven't started the show yet," Rebecca explained. "Don't be such a *nudge*, pestering me every minute."

Rebecca stood at the edge of the stoop, right at the top of the steps. She took a deep breath and began singing her favorite song. "Take me out to the ball game, take me out with the crowd . . ."

A few passersby turned to look, but they didn't stop. Rebecca kept singing. Maybe she just had to be patient. Surely a crowd would form soon. She sang louder. But when she finished, no one had stopped, and there were no pennies in Benny's cap.

Rebecca tilted the floppy brim on Mama's straw

hat at an angle, like Pearl White's hat. She cleared her throat and began singing at the top of her lungs.

> *I went to the animal fair,*
> *The birds and the beasts were there.*
> *The big baboon by the light of the moon*
> *Was combing his auburn hair.*

Benny hopped up and down, hooting and scratching his chest the way the organ grinder's monkey scratched his fur. A few people paused to watch as Rebecca belted out the end of the song.

> *The monkey he got drunk*
> *And climbed up the elephant's trunk,*
> *The elephant sneezed and fell on his knees,*
> *And what became of the monk,*
> *The monk, the monk, the monk?*

As Rebecca repeated "the monk" over and over, Benny flitted through the thin crowd. Rebecca saw a stout man drop a coin into the hat. Now she was getting somewhere! Maybe a few jokes would bring the people closer. Max had said, "If you make them laugh, your audience will love you."

Rebecca walked down a few steps and began sprinkling the sidewalk with imaginary powder. "Ask me what I'm doing," she whispered to Benny.

"Okay," Benny whispered back. "What are you doing?"

"Louder," Rebecca hissed through her teeth, pretending to look around nervously.

"What are you *doing*?" Benny yelled.

"I'm sprinkling lion powder!" Rebecca announced clearly.

"Lion powder?" asked Benny. "What's that for?"

The crowd drew closer and looked from Rebecca's hand to the steps. More people joined the group.

Rebecca sprinkled with renewed energy. This routine was going well. "Why, it keeps the lions away," she replied loudly.

Benny started laughing, and Rebecca had to prompt him with the next line. But Benny was quick. "I 'member," he insisted. "But there aren't any lions around here!" he shouted to the crowd. Then he pointed toward the front door. "'Cept for those ones up there!"

The audience chuckled. Benny was a little showman.

Rebecca delivered the punch line. "Well, then, you see how well it works!"

People began to laugh. Benny jumped into the gathering holding out his hat, and Rebecca heard the clink of coins. Suddenly, strong fingers pinched her ear.

"Youch!" she cried. She twisted around and saw Bubbie, who was furiously pulling her up the steps.

"You are shaming us in the neighborhood," Bubbie scolded. "Even Mr. Rossi sees you begging!" Rebecca caught a glimpse of the man in the basement apartment scowling at her through his window as Bubbie dragged her along.

"Let go," Rebecca pleaded. "What did I do wrong?"

"You get inside and think about it!" Bubbie said.

"Why is it okay for Max to earn money in a show, but it's not okay for me?"

"Max, Schmax!" Bubbie sputtered. "He doesn't earn two nickels to rub together. Such a man you don't want to be like!"

But Rebecca really *did* want to be a performer, just like Max. She couldn't see anything wrong with earning money by putting on a show.

Rebecca saw her brother pulling out his marbles.
His cap was still on the sidewalk. "Benny," she hissed
under her breath. "Bring the cap!"

Bubbie led Rebecca into the girls' bedroom and left,
closing the door firmly behind her. Sadie and Sophie
looked up from *Hamlet*.

"You're not ready for the stage yet," Sadie laughed,
"but the hat is really you!"

Rebecca's cheeks felt hot. "People liked my show,"
she said. "They even paid for it!" she added as Benny
burst into the room and dumped the pennies on her bed.
She counted six copper coins. It wasn't much, but it was
something. She tied the money into her handkerchief.

"I want some pennies, too!" Benny protested.

"It was my idea," Rebecca argued, "and my show."

"But I did the joke," Benny insisted. "And I got the
pennies." Rebecca dropped a penny into his hand.
"No fair!" he whined. "You've got more than me!"

"Oh, all right!" Rebecca gave him two more
pennies. It was better than having Bubbie come in
to settle it. Benny dashed off, and Rebecca looked
dismally at what was left. After all that effort, she
had just three cents.

Sadie closed her book with a dull thud that echoed in Rebecca's ears. "We're going to the park. How can anyone study in this madhouse?" A wayward curl at her forehead bounced like a coiled spring. Sophie always plastered her curl flat. It was one way to tell the twins apart.

Rebecca flopped onto her bed. The show had seemed like such a good idea, but Bubbie certainly didn't approve. *Were* the neighbors laughing at her? she wondered. It hardly mattered anyway, since she could never earn much money singing on the stoop. So far, the most she had earned at one time was the quarter she had gotten from Mrs. Berg.

Rebecca buried her pennies in her trunk, pushing aside the neatly folded doilies and linens stored inside. *Imagine saving all these until I'm grown-up,* she thought. She counted all the items she had made—ten pillow covers, seventeen doilies, six long table scarves, and twenty-four napkins. She couldn't use all those linens in her whole life! But seeing the piles of needlework gave her another idea. She packed several items into her calico bag until it bulged.

If Papa would just let her work in the store a few

more Saturdays, she'd earn all the money she needed.
In just a few weeks, she would stand next to her sisters
on Friday night and light candles herself. Everyone
would see how grown-up she was. Even Bubbie would
be proud of her then.

# Solving a Riddle

 month had passed, and Rebecca had worked with Papa every Saturday. Today the store was as busy as ever. Some customers browsed among the displays, some paid for their new shoes, and others sat and waited for Papa to fit them. No wonder he had to keep the store open on Saturdays.

Each week Rebecca had improved on her plan to earn money. Now she knew exactly what to do. While Papa bustled between his customers and the back room, she draped a few doilies and pillow covers over a chair. As the ladies strolled by, examining the latest styles, Rebecca hummed and rearranged her pieces.

"How lovely," commented a customer. She fingered a lacy table runner, the plumes on her hat swaying. "Now that so few girls make a trousseau, it's hard to find handmade items anywhere. My niece just announced her engagement, and this table runner would be a charming gift. Is it for sale?" the lady asked.

"Oh, no," Rebecca said. "I made these myself, and they take so long!"

The lady pulled a quarter from her purse and held it between her gloved thumb and forefinger. "Would this change your mind, dear?" she asked.

"I couldn't," Rebecca murmured. "Papa might be angry."

"It will be our little secret," the lady whispered as she added a dime.

Rebecca quickly folded the table runner into the customer's shopping bag and tucked the coins into her own bag. As Papa stepped out of the back room with a stack of shoe boxes, the lady put her finger to her lips. Rebecca smiled demurely.

This routine had been repeated many times over the past few Saturdays. She wasn't offering to sell her work, Rebecca told herself. If people insisted on buying, it wasn't because she had asked them. She didn't even bargain. She had discovered that people offered more money if you simply said an item wasn't for sale. When she brought her calico bag home each week, it was no longer bulging with doilies and napkins, but it was heavy with dimes, quarters, and half-dollars.

Rebecca replaced several pairs of unwanted shoes in their boxes, smoothed the rumpled tissue paper, and tried to avoid Papa's eyes. He really might be angry if he knew what she was doing. After all, people had come into the store to buy shoes, and she was taking their attention.

"What a fine helper you have," commented an elderly man buying a pair of dressy brogues. "Maybe someday the store will be called 'Rubin and Daughter.'"

Papa smiled proudly. "No, this young lady is going to be a teacher."

*Maybe*, Rebecca thought. *Or I might be an actress.*

Papa placed the man's box of shoes on the glass case near the cash register. Inside the case were a few dusty cans of shoe polish and wooden shoetrees to help shoes keep their shape. Rebecca thought doilies would be much prettier to display and sell. But how could she tell Papa without giving away her secret?

"You're awfully quiet this evening," Papa said as they walked home. "I guess being a working girl is more tiring than you realized."

But Rebecca wasn't tired. Her plan to sell her linens had worked better than she had expected. Now she had more than enough money to shop for candlesticks on Orchard Street. At first, her heart had skipped at the happy thought. But then she began to worry about whether she should be selling her trousseau. Her trunk was nearly empty now. Bubbie had been so proud of her needlework—she'd be very upset if she found out Rebecca had sold it.

And something else was bothering her even more. She couldn't stop thinking about Ana, who had to leave Russia soon. How could her cousin make such a long journey when she was weak and ill? Ana would need a lot of courage to face the dangerous escape.

"Papa," she asked, "is cousin Ana still sick? Is she coming to America soon?"

Papa gave her hand a squeeze. "Is that what's on your mind?" he asked. "I'm afraid I haven't heard any more news about Ana. I've been setting aside as much money as possible, but we still need a great deal more.

I'll send Uncle Jacob the ship tickets as soon as I can."

Rebecca swallowed, feeling uncertain. The last time she had offered her savings to Papa, he hadn't wanted her pennies. But now she had a lot more than twenty-seven cents. In fact, she thought she had enough for real silver candlesticks. If she used her money to buy them, she could finally light the candles every Friday night. She still wanted to light the candles as much as ever, but somehow the thought of buying her own candlesticks had lost its glow.

Rebecca's hand in Papa's felt hot and sweaty. Papa always said helping others was a mitzvah—something you should do. She remembered the day in the shoe store when Papa had said, "Your heart tells you the right thing to do." Rebecca's heart beat faster in her chest. *Instead of helping Ana, I've been thinking only of myself,* she realized. *I've got to give Papa the money I've earned so that he can buy the ship tickets as soon as possible.*

Rebecca was about to make her offer when a more troubling thought stopped her from saying a word. Papa would ask where she got the money. If she told him she had been selling her needlework in the store, he would be angry. And what would Bubbie and Mama say when they found out she had sold her trousseau? Rebecca's throat felt dry. She could never tell them what she had done!

When Rebecca and Papa turned in at their row house, Mr. Rossi was washing chalk from the sidewalk with a long-handled broom. A bucket of brown water stood in a soapy puddle near the stoop. Mr. Rossi cleaned the building in exchange for his rent, but Rebecca thought he acted as if he owned it.

"These kids is always drawing the chalk marks!" he complained. He glowered at Rebecca. "It's you girls making the squares for jumping!"

"*I* wasn't playing hopscotch, Mr. Rossi," Rebecca said. "I was working at my father's store today."

He wiggled his finger in her face. "Today, is not you. Tomorrow, maybe *is* you!"

What a grouch Mr. Rossi was! He lived alone and didn't like children at all. So what if the neighborhood girls chalked a hopscotch game on the sidewalk? It wasn't *his* sidewalk, thought Rebecca, and besides, the chalk marks would wash away as soon as it rained. But she couldn't waste time worrying about Mr. Rossi.

His problem with the chalk wasn't as important as her problem at all.

ᑀᑊᕙᔕᕗᒧᑊᒕ

All through dinner, thoughts about her empty trunk and Ana and the candlesticks chased each other around in Rebecca's head. Then a horrible thought crept into her mind. Uncle Jacob had said he didn't think Ana could survive another winter. What if her cousin got sicker? What if—what if she died?

*I've got to give my money to Papa before it's too late,* Rebecca thought. But how could she admit what she had done?

Rebecca barely looked up when there was a rhythmic tapping on the door and Max walked in.

"Moyshe," Grandpa said, "you're too late for dinner, but come sit."

Max lifted the lids off the pans on the stove. "First I'll help with the leftover blintzes," he said. "After all, I do want to help out around here."

Mama filled a plate and added a dollop of sour cream. Max sat down and ate hungrily.

"Do you feel like tea?" Bubbie asked him.

"Well, let me see." Max pinched his arm. "No, I don't think I do feel like tea. How about Benny?" He pinched Benny's nose. "Nope, he doesn't feel like tea, either. As for Beckie," he said, pinching her cheek, "you don't feel like tea at all. More like a rosy peach."

A murmur of laughter rippled around the table. Rebecca couldn't even smile. She knew in her heart what she had to do—but why did it have to be so hard? She thought again of Ana and the courage it would take to escape to America. If Rebecca was going to help her cousin, she would have to show some courage, too.

She twisted her napkin in her hand. "Papa," she began in a whispery voice, "I—"

But Max already had Papa's ear. "Believe it or not, I didn't come by just to sponge a dinner from you," he said. "I saw a newsreel at the theater today. The war is spreading fast, and fewer ships are leaving Europe. There's no time to spare if you want to get Jacob and his family out."

Papa scowled. "I know, Max," he snapped. "I'm doing the best I can."

"You don't understand," Max said, pulling a wallet from his pocket. "I really did come here to help."

A wide grin spread across his face. "Remember the audition I had a few weeks ago? Well, you are now looking at Max Shepard, movie actor."

Rebecca stared at Max in amazement. Imagine, a movie actor in her family!

Grandpa lifted his bushy eyebrows. "So, it's a good job?"

"The best!" Max said. "I'll be working steady and getting paid every week. In fact, I got my first paycheck yesterday." Bubbie gasped as he pulled five crisp ten-dollar bills from his wallet.

"The movie business pays pretty good dough," Max said. "No more borrowing money for me! I can pay off my debts and look for my own apartment now." Max handed Papa the money. "I hope this helps buy your brother's tickets."

Papa blinked as if he couldn't believe his eyes. Then he shook his head and tried to give back the money. "You don't have to do this," he said. "After all, it's not your brother."

But Max wouldn't take it. "Consider it repayment for all the money you've loaned me over the years," Max said. He winked at Mama. "And all the dinners you're going to feed me, now that I'm living here in the city."

Papa shook Max's hand and accepted his gift. "This will go a long way," he admitted. "I'll borrow the rest of what we need. It will just take a while to pay it off." Mama leaned over and gave Max a kiss on the cheek.

"And there's one more thing," Max added. "Is it really true that there are people in this family who have yet to see a moving picture?"

"You can put me on that list," Mama said with a smile at Rebecca.

"This is my last weekend working as an usher at the Strand," Max said. "If you come to the matinee tomorrow, I'll get the whole family in free."

Rebecca could barely believe it. There seemed to be no end to Max's surprises.

Bubbie and Grandpa exchanged nervous glances.

"Don't worry," Max reassured them. "It's a Charlie Chaplin comedy, *Dough and Dynamite*. It's perfect for everyone—even Benny. You'll laugh until your sides hurt!" He nudged Rebecca. "And there's an episode of *The Perils of Pauline* with Pearl White."

How Rebecca had dreamed of seeing a moving picture! But tonight Max's surprise didn't make her

happy. When Papa and Mama learned what she had
done, they would make her stay home, she was sure.
Blinking back tears, Rebecca slipped from the room
and returned with her calico bag.

"I have something to tell you, Papa," she said.
"Please don't be angry." She took handfuls of change
from her bag and dropped them onto the table. Nickels,
dimes, quarters, and heavy half-dollars clinked into a
pile. Everyone stared at her.

Mama's lips were set in a thin line. "Rebecca Rubin,
where did you get this money?"

Rebecca's face burned. She tried not to look at Bubbie. "I—I sold my needlework at the shoe store."

"*Oy vey!*" Bubbie cried. "Your trousseau—such a
shame!"

"I'm sorry," Rebecca said, her eyes downcast.

"How did you do it?" asked Sadie.

"I brought my linens and doilies to the store, and
ladies offered me money for them." Tears of shame
filled Rebecca's eyes.

Mama shook her head slowly, as if she couldn't
believe what Rebecca had done. "Why did you do
this?" she asked.

Rebecca answered in a near whisper. "I wanted to buy candlesticks."

"For what you need candlesticks?" Bubbie asked. "One pair isn't enough?"

Rebecca hung her head. "*I* wanted to light candles on Shabbos, too."

Everyone sat in silence. Rebecca wished she could make herself disappear.

Then Mama came over and lifted Rebecca's chin. "Always so impatient," she sighed. "I was impatient once, too. I thought I'd never be old enough to welcome the Sabbath. I pretended to light candles using twigs stuck in the ground." She wrapped her arms around Rebecca and held her.

Now that her secret was out, tears of relief and regret rolled down Rebecca's cheeks. "The more things I sold," she sobbed, "and the more money I earned, the less important the candlesticks seemed."

"So," Papa said, "that's what brought on all the secret deals in the shoe store."

Rebecca blinked in astonishment. "You knew I was selling my things?" she asked. "And you aren't angry?"

Papa shrugged. "When your daughter is a successful

American businesswoman, what can a father do except sit back and watch?"

Rebecca wiped her eyes and looked at Papa. "What I really want is for Ana and her family to come. I've got more than eight dollars. I know that's not nearly enough for a ticket, but maybe I could sell some more things, and you won't need to borrow so much money."

Suddenly, Sophie spoke up. Her voice was filled with excitement. "Sadie and I have oodles of napkins and doilies and linens. Let's sell some of those, too!" This time it was Sadie who nodded in agreement, her curl bouncing.

Rebecca's face brightened. "You know, Papa," she said, "the display case near the cash register is wasted with shoe polish in it. Let's put the linens there!"

Bubbie sat silently. Now she looked thoughtful. "If people pay to have doilies," she said, "I have a trunkful. And tablecloths, bed covers, fancy shawls . . . all sitting in a dark trunk. So, I'll sell a little, too! It's a mitzvah."

Grandpa patted Bubbie's arm. "After all, you're already married. A trousseau you don't need!"

For the first time in weeks, Rebecca's heart felt light. Papa didn't mind what she had done. Mama understood why she had sold her needlework. And Bubbie wasn't angry. She was even going to help!

"If this works," Papa said, "we'll pay for the tickets in no time." He put his hand on Rebecca's shoulder. "But you, young lady, will have to be in charge of handling the merchandise. Do you think you can arrange the display case?"

"I know I can!" Rebecca exclaimed.

Max stood up. In a deep stage voice he said, "In the true Russian tradition, the youngest daughter has solved the family's riddle of how to get the money for ship tickets." He raised his glass of tea. "Here's to Rebecca!"

Bubbie got up and came over to Rebecca. She unhooked the pin with the leaping hare from her collar and fastened it to Rebecca's dress. "Keep this, to remember that you are our own Clever Karina."

Rebecca hugged Bubbie. "Just as long as I don't have to marry the tsar!" she said.

"Don't worry," Mama laughed. "He'd never have you without a trousseau!"

# Welcome to America

he days passed slowly as Rebecca waited for cousin Ana's ship to land. She had been worrying about Ana ever since Uncle Jacob's telegram had arrived a few weeks ago. *Escaped Russia with great difficulty. Arriving New York 8 November 1914.* Ana had been ill before she left. Was her health the "great difficulty" Uncle Jacob had mentioned?

The day of their arrival finally came. Rebecca squinted through the gray fog that blanketed New York Harbor. She could barely see the outline of the brick buildings at Ellis Island. That was where immigrants came when they first arrived in New York. Papa was there now, meeting Uncle Jacob and his family.

Rebecca tugged nervously at her skirt. Had her cousin made it through the difficult voyage? If only Ana survived the journey safely, Rebecca was sure they would become as close as sisters. As the wind began to scatter the thin gray wisps of fog, she saw a small ferryboat chugging across the harbor. Behind it, the Statue of Liberty stood out against the clouds.

"Do you think Ana's on that ferry?" she asked, turning to her family. "We've been waiting for hours."

Rebecca's grandparents huddled together against the wind. Bubbie drew her kerchief tighter around her head, and Grandpa pulled his scarf up around his neck. Little Benny stood on a bench, watching the boats, and Victor held on to Benny's collar so that he wouldn't tumble over.

"It takes a long time to get through Immigration," Mama told Rebecca.

Grandpa shook his head, remembering. "So many people! Such lines! We shuffled into line to get off the ship. We stood in line to go into the building, *schlepping* everything we owned. Then another line while we walked up those steep stairs, praying nobody thought we looked sick."

"I should think *everyone* would feel sick after two weeks sailing across the ocean," said Rebecca's sister Sadie.

Sophie looked sympathetically at her grandparents. "You must have been so anxious."

Bubbie nodded. "If inspectors thought something was wrong, they might not let us into America."

"When we were on the ship," Mama said, "other passengers warned us about passing through Immigration. Just because you land in New York, it doesn't mean you can live here. The officials keep out anyone who has a serious illness. If they think you have a problem, they mark a letter on your coat with chalk. An *E* means you might have an eye disease. *H* means you might have a heart problem. There's a long list."

Rebecca had heard lots of stories about Ellis Island from her friends at school. When immigrants had a disease that could spread, officials sent them back to the country they came from.

Rebecca remembered what her friend Rose Krensky had told her about immigrants who were sick when they arrived. "*Contagious disease*, they call it," Rose said. "You got one, you go back. That's it. And the ship company has to pay for your ticket." Rebecca tried to forget about Rose's words. She could only hope Ana was well enough to climb the stairs at Ellis Island.

Mama's cousin Max paced along the walkway. "I've got an idea," Max said, flashing his sparkling smile. "Let's practice a little welcoming song to greet the family when they step off the ferry. We'll sing 'You're a Grand Old Flag.'" He started humming.

"I know some of it," Rebecca said. "I heard it on the phonograph at the candy store."

"She buys one soda," Victor teased, "and hangs around for an hour, sucking up the music along with the drink!"

Max started singing softly. Rebecca knew the chorus, and so did the twins. Her sisters linked their arms as they chimed in. "You're a grand old flag, you're a high-flying flag, and forever in peace may you wave ... "

When Rebecca no longer knew the words, she quietly hummed along. She listened carefully as Max sang. He made every word sound exciting! "You're the emblem of the land I love, the home of the *free* and the *brave* ... " He emphasized some of the words, giving the song more rhythm. Bubbie nodded in time to the music, and Grandpa tapped his foot. Benny marched around them in a small circle, saluting each time he passed Max.

A loud horn blast whistled through the air, and Benny covered his ears. The ferry pulled up to the dock, smoke belching from its smokestack. Rebecca stretched up on her toes, trying to see the passengers on deck. Hundreds of people crowded at the railing in strange-looking clothing—rough black coats, long scarves that fell past their knees, odd flat caps and summer straw hats. Their arms were weighed down with feather beds, quilts, and bulging carpetbags, yet their tired faces glowed with excitement.

"Another boatload of new Americans," Max smiled. He nudged Mama. "Just like we were, not so long ago."

"There's Papa!" Rebecca exclaimed. She jumped up and down, waving in his direction. Papa had gone to Ellis Island to sign papers proving that Uncle Jacob and his family had someone to help them settle in America. Rebecca searched the crowd anxiously, trying to guess which girl was her cousin. Even if Ana was sick, the immigration officials wouldn't send her back to Russia alone, would they?

"Start singing," Max directed them.

Above the din of shuffling feet and shouted greet-

ings in many languages, Rebecca sang with all her
might.

"Over here!" Mama called, and Rebecca saw Papa
standing next to his brother. Rebecca thought she would
have recognized Uncle Jacob anywhere. Although he
looked older than Papa, with streaks of gray in his hair
and beard, he looked very much like her father. Beside
him, Aunt Fanya looked pale and weary. Her shoulders
slumped, and her eyes were rimmed with dark circles.
A boy a bit taller than Victor waved his hand toward
them. He must be either Michael or Josef.

Then Rebecca saw a girl about her own age, right
behind Aunt Fanya. It had to be Ana, but she looked
nothing like Rebecca had imagined. Her cheeks were
smudged with streaks of dirt. Her face looked thin and
drawn under her wool scarf, but the rest of her bulged,
and her clothes pulled at their buttons. Like the other
immigrants, she had a large passenger tag pinned to
her coat, which flapped in the breeze.

Rebecca glanced at the crowd behind them. Where
was Ana's other brother? Perhaps he was further back
in the crush of people.

Suddenly Max's voice trailed off. The musical

greeting floated away as the families embraced each other.

"Thank heavens you're here!" Mama said as she hugged Aunt Fanya. Then she looked anxiously at the rest of the family. "Where is—?"

In Yiddish, Aunt Fanya cried, "They've taken Josef!" She began to sob, louder and louder until she was wailing. Strangers paused to look and then quickly turned away. Uncle Jacob put his arm around her shoulders, as if holding her up. Ana clutched her mother's arm and began to cry.

"Josef fell on the ship and hurt his leg badly," Papa explained. "He was limping when he passed through the inspection point, and the officials marked his coat with an *L*. They separated him from the others and took him away."

It didn't seem possible. Rebecca had worried about Ana making the voyage safely, but she had never imagined that someone else in the family might become sick. Now the officials were holding Josef on Ellis Island and might send him back to Russia! She thought about the mark on Josef's coat.

"Does *L* mean 'limp'?" she asked Papa.

"It means 'lame.' The doctors are afraid Josef won't be able to walk." A deep frown creased Papa's forehead, but he tried to sound hopeful. He turned to his brother and added in Yiddish, "We'll come back tomorrow and see about getting Josef released. If all goes well, the Ellis Island doctors can treat him and he'll be better soon."

Aunt Fanya tugged weakly at Papa's arm. "Don't let them send him back!" Her eyes were filled with fear.

"Don't worry," Papa said gently. "I'll go to the Hebrew Immigrant Aid Society. They'll know what to do."

Rebecca offered Ana her handkerchief. "Don't cry," she said in Yiddish. "Papa will help." But she knew from what Rose had told her that getting Josef through Immigration wouldn't be easy.

Mama took the ship tags off the family's clothing, and they all set off down the street, with bundles clutched to their chests. Cousin Max held Benny's hand and carried a big brass samovar under one strong arm. Rebecca's family had a samovar from Russia, too. Samovars were used for making tea. Grandpa had always told Rebecca that a samovar was a family's treasure and something they tried not to leave behind.

Papa and Uncle Jacob carried a wicker trunk between them. As they walked, Papa explained how horseless trolleys worked. Mama told Aunt Fanya about cooking on a gas stove. Victor tried to explain the game of baseball to Michael, batting at the air to demonstrate.

As always, the twins walked together, talking and giggling, but for once, Rebecca didn't mind. She usually hated it when her sisters left her out, but now she had Ana by her side. She balanced a heavy bundle against her chest and hooked her arm through Ana's, pointing out a huge theater with glittering lights.

"We have movies here," she said. "You watch the actors moving on a screen instead of on a stage." Ana's large brown eyes grew wider. Rebecca had so much to share with her cousin and could barely contain her happiness now that she had arrived. Although she was concerned about Josef, she was relieved that Ana's health was better. With fresh food from the markets, Ana would grow stronger every day. From now on, they would be together all the time.

When they entered their building, a cat dashed from the entrance down into the basement. "That's Pasta," Rebecca told Ana. "She belongs to Mr. Rossi, who takes care of the building. He says Pasta is the only cat who likes spaghetti more than chasing mice!"

Ana frowned. "Not know these words," she said. Before Rebecca could explain, Mama spoke.

"I know you all want baths," said Mama with a smile as they crowded into the apartment. "Louis," she said to Papa, "take your brother and Michael to the bath house." She handed Papa two towels, a small cake of soap, and a neatly tied bundle of fresh clothes. Then she pulled the metal washtub from under the sink and set it in the middle of the kitchen. She started filling a bucket with hot water.

"Hot water pours from the faucet?" Aunt Fanya marveled. "Right in the kitchen?"

Mama nodded. "The ladies will have their baths here. Everyone else, scoot!"

Bubbie herded the rest of the family upstairs. "I'll make tea," she said, "and I've got a big plate of rugalach." Max licked his lips.

Rebecca could wait until later for Bubbie's flaky cinnamon pastry. She wasn't going to leave Ana now. "I'll help with the baths," she announced.

Ana untied her scarf, and Rebecca was delighted to

see that her cousin's hair was the same rich brown shade as her own. They already looked almost like twins!

Layers of blouses, skirts, and sweaters lay beneath Ana's bulging buttons. By the time she had shed everything except her slip, Ana looked like a scrawny chicken that had lost all its feathers.

"We not have room to pack many things," Ana said in halting English. "I wear all clothes."

"How did you learn to speak English?" Rebecca asked. "You speak very well."

"In Russia, we have boarder who teach us English," Ana said proudly. "I learn fastly."

Mama looked doubtfully at the pile of dirty clothes. Rebecca knew that puffy peasant blouses and long skirts with bands of embroidery along the hem would mark Ana as a *greenhorn*. That was the insulting term some Americans called newcomers just off the boat.

"Instead of washing these," Mama said, "I think you'll want to replace them with American clothes."

Aunt Fanya looked horrified. "Throw away clothes?"

Mama nodded. "I'm sure the ship was riddled with lice."

Rebecca shuddered at the thought of bugs crawling in her clothes. "I've got the perfect dress for Ana," she exclaimed. "In fact, with hand-me-downs from the twins, I've got two of everything! Ana and I can dress exactly alike."

"Now you're *Amerikanka*," Mama said to Fanya. "An American. The first thing to do is dress like one." She splashed a final bucket of hot water into the tub.

Ana stepped in and began scrubbing away weeks of grime and sour ship smells. "On ship, we must wash with salty seawater," she said. "Now water in tub is Ana soup!"

Rebecca laughed at the joke. Ana really did speak English pretty well. Rebecca sat down next to her aunt. "Now you should have an American name," she said. "May I call you Aunt Fannie?"

"Fannie," repeated her aunt. In Yiddish, she said, "I like this American name. I will dress American, and learn to speak it, too—if I stay." She twisted the fringes on her scarf and looked down sadly. "If Josef is sent back, we all go back together."

Ana stopped scrubbing, and her eyes brimmed with tears. "We can't go back to Russia," she said hoarsely. "It's too far. Papa can't work there, and Michael and Josef have to hide in the house from the tsar's soldiers."

Aunt Fannie began to cry, her shoulders shaking. Mama put her arms around her. "Even if there were enough money for new tickets," she said gently, "there's no life for you in Russia anymore." She looked steadily at Aunt Fannie. "I'm afraid there's no going back."

A cold feeling grew in Rebecca's stomach. The pile of clothes seemed like the Russian life Ana and her family had to throw away. But if Russia wasn't safe, how would Josef survive if he was sent back alone?

# A Yiddish Mistake

ebecca felt warm and cozy in her bed, and when she opened her eyes, she remembered why. There was Ana, sound asleep beside her, with Rebecca's wooden doll, Beckie, smiling between them. *Now I've got a twin, just like my sisters,* she thought happily. She patted Ana's shoulder.

"Wake up," she said. "We're going to school!" Ana stretched sleepily, kicking Rebecca's ankles, but Rebecca didn't mind. "We can dress exactly alike," she announced. She pulled matching skirts and sweaters from the closet and laid out stockings, shoes, and hair ribbons. Rebecca helped her cousin tie her stockings at her thighs.

"Don't be nervous about school," Rebecca said. "We're going to stay together the whole time." She brushed out her cousin's hair and tied on a fluffy bow. Then Ana did the same for her before they went into the kitchen.

"You two must think you're looking into a mirror," Mama exclaimed. "You look so alike, it's like having two sets of twins in the house!" Rebecca beamed, and Ana gave a shy smile.

Sadie urged Benny up from the chairs he slept on each night. Papa always pulled two chairs together for him and covered them with soft blankets. Now, every chair was needed at the table.

The apartment was crowded with the new family. Victor usually slept on the couch in the parlor, but he had let Michael take that spot. Instead, Victor had spent the night on a feather bed that Mama spread on the floor. Uncle Jacob and Aunt Fannie had slept upstairs in Bubbie and Grandpa's parlor, but they came down to help Michael and Ana go to school.

Mama set glasses of coffee mixed with milk on the table beside a heaping plate of sweet rolls. "When Josef comes, we'll put another feather bed on the floor," she said.

*If he comes,* Rebecca thought.

Aunt Fannie looked at the coffee and rolls. "No

tea?" she asked. "And what about soup?"

Rebecca giggled. "We don't have soup for breakfast in America! And we drink coffee in the morning." She stirred a lump of sugar into a glass of warm coffee milk and handed it to Ana.

After one sip, Ana smiled. "Is tasty!" she assured her mother. "America *is* land of milk and honey!"

As soon as one person finished eating, Mama washed the dishes and quickly refilled them for someone else. Rebecca could barely move around the crowded kitchen, and there was no place for her to sit. As she stood near the warm stove eating her roll, there was a knock at the door. Papa opened it to find Mr. Rossi scowling at him.

"*Scusi*, Mr. Rubin," the janitor said, "but you know is against the rules to take in boarders here."

Papa appeared calm as he answered, but Rebecca saw his mustache twitch in anger. "Don't worry, Mr. Rossi, these aren't boarders. This is my brother and his family. They just got to America yesterday. They'll be getting settled on their own very soon." Papa smiled slightly. "You know how hard it is when you first arrive in New York!"

Mr. Rossi only grumbled. "A few days, okay, but no more. Otherwise, I have to report to the landlord. I come check again. I'm sorry, but it's my job." He left, and Papa closed the door.

"Where will we go?" Aunt Fannie asked, speaking in Yiddish.

"I'm going to start looking for a job today," Uncle Jacob said. "We don't want to cause trouble for you, Louis. I'm a good cabinetmaker, and I hope to find work and a place to live as quickly as possible."

"You'll stay here as long as necessary," Papa reassured him. "If we have trouble with Mr. Rossi, I'll speak to the landlord myself."

"What a grouch," Rebecca said under her breath. Mr. Rossi always seemed to be griping about something. He even complained that Pasta didn't catch enough mice.

Still, she couldn't help feeling a bit worried. Now he was causing trouble for Ana and her family. Rebecca had waited so long for Ana to arrive, and if Mr. Rossi made them move, she would lose her new twin. Mr. Rossi couldn't make them leave, could he?

Mama gave each of the children a lunch box and

handed Aunt Fannie her scarf. "I'll help you register Michael and Ana at school," she said. "Be sure to bring their immigration papers along."

Uncle Jacob patted his son on the head and beamed. "The best thing in America is free schools that everyone can attend," he said. "I hope Michael can keep going to school and not have to work."

"He's too young to have a job," Papa explained. "In New York, children must stay in school until they are fourteen years old."

Uncle Jacob sighed. "Thirteen or fourteen," he said, "makes no difference. If Josef can't help us earn a living, then Michael will have to work."

"Well, let's hope for the best," Papa said. He turned to Mama. "When you take Fanya to register the children, don't let the school put them with the first-graders just because their English isn't perfect. They'll catch on quickly."

"Please make sure Ana stays in Miss Maloney's classroom with me," Rebecca pleaded. "Ana and I are going to be like a new pair of shoes—always together!"

Outside, Mama and Aunt Fannie led the way, while Victor, Michael, and the girls followed in the brisk morning air. "Look, there's my friend Rose!" Rebecca said. "She moved here from Russia last year." They hurried to catch up, and Rebecca introduced her cousin.

Rose's hair was in tight braids, with a blue ribbon tied at the end of each one. "Ever been to school?" Rose asked Ana.

Ana shook her head. "At home my papa teaches me to read and figure numbers. But I'm speak English."

Rose wagged her finger in the air. "I'll give you a piece of advice. Don't speak a single word of Yiddish in school."

"Piece of advice?" Ana repeated. "Piece of paper, I know. Piece of bread, this I know. What is 'piece of advice'?"

"Oh, brother," Rose laughed. "You're going to have your hands full, Rebecca."

As the girls arrived at school, Ana hung back. "Is so big," she whispered, gazing up at the huge brick and stone building that nearly spanned a city block.

"Welcome to P.S. 64," Rebecca said. "The *P* stands for 'public,' which means everyone who lives here can attend for free. And the *S* just stands for 'school.'"

"In New York," Rose explained, "the neighborhood schools have numbers instead of names. We're lucky to go to P.S. 64, because it's nearly new."

Rebecca took Ana's hand and led her to the girls' entrance. "This is where we go in," she explained. "The boys have a different door. In the classroom there's a closet to hang up our things. You and I can share a hook."

Miss Maloney stood at the door, her hair in a puffy pompadour and her shirtwaist and skirt crisply pressed. Mama and Aunt Fannie waited politely to one side while the girls lined up.

"Silence, please," the teacher reminded the chattering girls. "Proceed into the school like young ladies."

Rebecca put her finger to her lips, and her cousin understood right away. Ana was smart, Rebecca thought, and would quickly catch on to the school routine.

As the girls filed in, Miss Maloney put her hand on Ana's shoulder. "And who are you?"

"That's my cousin," Rebecca explained. "She just came from Russia yesterday. She's exactly my age, Miss Maloney. I can help her if she stays with me."

The teacher looked uncertainly at Ana. "Your parents must register you at the office," she said. "You might belong in the class for immigrants who need to learn English."

Mama stepped forward and introduced herself and Aunt Fannie. "I'll help Mrs. Rubin with all the paperwork," she said, "and we expect Ana will do fine in a regular class, as long as Rebecca is nearby to help her out."

"I'm speak English," Ana declared. She cleared her throat. "My name is Ana Rubin. I have nine years. I can write English alphabet."

Miss Maloney crossed her arms and tapped her finger thoughtfully. Then she turned to Mama. "We'll try it for a few days, but if it doesn't work out, she'll have to go into a lower grade, or the special class." She looked at Rebecca. "Help your cousin learn the routine, but I want no unnecessary talking, and you must speak only in English. Otherwise Ana will never learn."

"I'll take care of her," Rebecca promised as Mama and Aunt Fannie set off for the school's main office. Rebecca was filled with excitement as she showed her cousin where to store her lunch box. Ana was going to be in school with her every day!

Miss Maloney moved one of the students so that the girls could sit side by side at the wooden desks bolted to the floor. She made a quick check to see that the students' hands and faces were clean and their hair neatly combed. The pupils showed her their clean white handkerchiefs. Then Miss Maloney stood at the front of the room.

"Class," she began, and the students sat up straight with their hands folded on their desks. "Since it's Monday morning, and your minds have probably been quite idle during the weekend, we shall begin with some arithmetic teasers. Leo Berg, you are class monitor this week."

Leo walked around importantly and handed out blank paper at the beginning of each row of desks. When he reached Ana's row, he smirked at her. "Greenie," he said under his breath.

Ana didn't understand what Leo had said and didn't know it was an insult. She gave him a friendly smile. Rebecca fumed. Leo was so nasty!

Ana leaned over and whispered, "What is 'teaser'?"

Rebecca tried to explain quietly. "Miss Maloney

gives us numbers to add and subtract. She does it out loud, very fast. We have to do the problem in our heads and then write down the answer." Ana looked puzzled.

Miss Maloney began the exercise, speaking rapidly. "Three plus five, minus two, plus six." The students all wrote down their answers, except for Ana. She tapped Rebecca's arm as Miss Maloney launched into the next problem. Rebecca tried to ignore her cousin and concentrate, but by the time Miss Maloney had gotten halfway through the new problem, Rebecca was impossibly lost. She had to leave the answer blank.

"Just add and subtract each number in your head," she explained again. But Ana still didn't understand. Maybe she didn't know the meaning of the words "add" and "subtract," Rebecca thought. There was only one way to make it clear. Covering her mouth and whispering softly, Rebecca began to explain the exercise in Yiddish. She hadn't spoken more than three words when Miss Maloney slapped her ruler against the desk. Rebecca was so startled, she nearly jumped out of her shoes.

"Rebecca Rubin," Miss Maloney said. "Come up here immediately."

Rebecca approached the teacher's large oak desk.
"I only needed to give her the directions—"

But Miss Maloney wouldn't listen. "You know the
rules," she said. "There is no place in this school for any
language except English." She took the dunce cap from
a shelf and plopped it on Rebecca's head.

Rebecca walked slowly to the tall stool in the corner
of the room, in front of everyone. Her face burned with
shame. Leo snickered, and his friends joined in. Soon
the entire class was laughing at her. When Rebecca
dared to look up, she saw Ana giggling and pointing
at the dunce cap.

Her heart sank. Even her cousin was making fun
of her! It was the worst punishment Rebecca could
imagine. Only Rose looked on with sympathy.

At lunch, Rebecca could barely eat. How could her
cousin have laughed at her? When Ana complained
about the food Mama had given them, Rebecca was out
of patience.

Ana frowned at her bagel. "In Russia we eat bagels
when somebody die."

"Bagels aren't just for funerals," Rebecca said curtly.
Maybe Ana was afraid it would be bad luck to eat a

bagel while Josef was sick at Ellis Island, but Rebecca
was too angry to care. "Don't be superstitious," she
snapped.

Ana looked confused. She clearly did not understand what Rebecca meant about being superstitious,
but she chewed her bagel without another word.

"Greenie! Greenie!" taunted Leo and his friends as
they passed by. "Yiddish-talking greenie!"

Rebecca jumped up and yelled back, "Meanie! Meanie!
Big fat wienie!" Wienie was short for wienerwurst, a
German sausage. That was a good name for Leo, thought
Rebecca with satisfaction.

Rose pulled her down. "Ignore them," she said.
"You'll only get into more trouble. How many mistakes
do you want to make today?"

Rebecca turned her back on the boys. "Even Ana
laughed at me," she muttered to Rose, still smarting
from the shame. "And I spoke Yiddish to help her!"

"Ana saw the others laughing and thought it must
be a joke," Rose explained. "She doesn't know what a
dunce cap is."

"What Ana not know?" Rebecca's cousin asked.

"The pointy hat Miss Maloney put on Rebecca

is called a dunce cap," Rose told her. "*Dunce* means 'stupid.' It's a punishment for breaking the rules. Rebecca broke the rules by speaking Yiddish in school."

Ana turned pale. "I *not* know!" she protested. "I am sorry, Rebecca. Don't be mad on me."

Rebecca forced a little smile. She didn't want to be angry with her cousin. She wanted to be as close as twins, but now she realized that it wasn't always going to be easy. Even Sadie and Sophie argued sometimes.

"School is difficult," Ana sighed. "My English not so good."

"Don't worry," Rose told her as they finished eating. "I didn't even know American letters when I first came. Now English is as easy for me as Yiddish. And you're lucky Miss Maloney didn't change your name." She closed her lunch box, and they headed back to their classroom.

"Get different name at school?" Ana asked.

"Oh, sure," Rose said. "Teachers do it all the time. In Russia, my name was Rifka." Ana nodded as if she knew that name. "But on the first day of school, they call me Rose. I was afraid to tell my parents. Then one day the teacher sends home a note. My mother reads it and says, 'Who is this Rose?' When I tell her it's me, she gets so mad!" Rose shrugged. "At home, I'm still Rifka, but here, I am Rose."

Ana shook her head. "I not like to have two names," she said.

As the girls settled down at their desks, Rebecca thought about Aunt Fannie. Was it wrong to give someone an American name? Her aunt had seemed pleased when Rebecca suggested the name Fannie. Her grandfather wanted to be called "Grandpa" instead of the Yiddish word, *Zayda*. And Max had changed his own name from Moyshe. Maybe it was only wrong when it wasn't your choice. How hard it must be to move to another country!

Miss Maloney smoothed her white shirtwaist and clasped her hands primly. "Boys and girls, our class has been chosen to present the morning assembly on Friday. The school has received a new American flag, and we will recite some poems to honor the occasion. Who can tell me how many stars are on the new flag, and why?"

Sarah Goldstein's hand shot into the air. She stood

up when Miss Maloney called on her. "In 1912, Arizona and New Mexico became states. Now there are 48 stars on the flag."

"That is correct, Sarah," said the teacher. She pointed to the poetry book she kept on her desk. "Tomorrow I will assign each of you a poem about the flag. You must memorize it by Thursday."

Lucy Valenti raised her hand and asked, "Can we sing a song, too?"

"There's no time for the class to learn a song," Miss Maloney said.

The class groaned with disappointment. "Oh, *please*, Miss Maloney," several students begged.

Miss Maloney thought for a moment. "It might be a good ending to the program. If one of you knows a good patriotic song, I'll consider it," she said. "We'll audition tomorrow, and I'll choose one singer only."

How wonderful it would be to sing on the stage, in front of the entire school! All afternoon Rebecca wondered which song she could prepare by tomorrow. Maybe she could learn the song Max had sung when Ana arrived. It was about a flag, and she already knew some of it.

When school ended for the day, several excited girls crowded together.

"I'm going to sing 'The Star-Spangled Banner,'" Sarah said. "It's all about the flag."

"I'll sing 'Yankee Doodle Dandy,'" Lucy chimed in. "It's not about the flag, but it's very patriotic."

"What means 'patriotic'?" Ana asked.

"That's easy," said Sarah. "It means you love your country and would do anything to defend it."

Ana looked confused. "I love land of Russia," she said, "but I never love tsar, and my brothers won't go in Russian army to fight."

"But now you love America," said Rebecca.

"Maybe someday," Ana said, "if America lets my brother Josef stay. How can Immigration men send him back to Russia just because leg is hurt? Is not right."

Rebecca had to agree. It *wasn't* fair to hold Josef. If he had injured his leg *after* he had landed in New York, no one would think of sending him back to Russia. But Ana was here to stay, and Rebecca hoped she would love her new country. Maybe being part of the assembly would make her feel more American. Rebecca would try to help.

# Music for a Song

~~~ CHAPTER 8 ~~~

 he girls all left school together, but Rebecca kept walking after her friends turned the corner for home. "I've got some shopping to do," she announced to Ana.

"You have money for buying?" Ana asked.

Rebecca jingled four pennies in the pocket of her sweater. She had told Mama she might treat Ana to a seltzer, but she could do that another day. As long as Mr. Rossi didn't cause trouble, Ana would be living with her for a long time, and today Rebecca needed something important.

"I've got to find the words and music to the song I want to sing at school," she said. "Just wait till you see all the pushcarts on Orchard Street. You can buy anything there. Each peddler sells something different. Pickles, fish, apples, pots and pans, cloth, hats—and music!"

The sun had warmed the afternoon air, and the girls strolled arm in arm. "That's Mr. Goldberg's candy shop," Rebecca said, pointing to a store with a striped awning over the front window and displays of candy-covered almonds and fancy chocolates. "He makes the best egg creams and plays the best music."

"What is egg cream?" Ana asked.

Rebecca squeezed her cousin's arm. "Oh, Ana, you're in for a treat. I'll take you when I get my allowance next Saturday. An egg cream is a chocolate-flavored soda. There's no egg in it, or cream," she explained, "but there's milk, and it has a big, bubbly top. It's smooth!"

"Smooth?" Ana repeated.

Rebecca smiled, thinking of how often her older sisters used the word. "*Smooth* means 'modern and wonderful,' all at once!"

"American way of speaking is strange," Ana observed. "Smooth means wonderful, and egg cream has no egg and no cream!" The girls giggled.

They walked until they came closer to the towering tenement buildings that crowded the Lower East Side. Ana stood still. "Is dark here," she said. "Not smooth."

"Don't worry," Rebecca reassured her. But Ana

didn't look convinced. Horse-drawn wagons and carts
crowded the streets, and horse droppings littered the
road, their foul smell rising in the air. Boys in large-
brimmed caps pitched bottle tops against a tall stoop.
They punched and jostled each other, laughing loudly.
As the girls walked farther the crowds grew thicker,
and soon it seemed to Rebecca as if she and Ana were
pushing against every person who had ever come to
America. Ana gripped Rebecca's arm when a train
clattered by on elevated tracks with a deafening roar.

"People live here?" Ana asked, peering into the
dark, open hallway of a tenement building. Smells of
boiled cabbage filled the air.

"Bubbie, Grandpa, and Mama lived near here
when they first came to America," Rebecca said.
"The rent is cheap." She pointed high up at a sooty
window behind a fire escape. "Mama and Papa lived
right there when they first got married, and even after
Sadie, Sophie, and Victor were born." Rebecca was
glad they now lived blocks away in their row house,
with large windows facing the front and the back.
Even on the hottest days, fresh air moved through
the apartment. "Don't worry," Rebecca reassured her

cousin. "You're not going to live here—just shop."

As they turned onto Orchard Street, the din of many voices rose about them almost as loud as the roar of the train. Peddlers shouted what they had to sell, and shoppers touched, squeezed, argued, bargained, and bought.

"Listen!" Ana shouted. "I hear Yiddish!" Her face lit up with pleasure.

"Sure," Rebecca laughed. "Practically everyone here speaks Yiddish."

So many carts lined the street that there was room for no other traffic than the people who trudged along on foot. Women carried large baskets or oilcloth bags bulging with potatoes, cabbages, and carrots. Knots of men stood and talked, gesturing with their hands.

"What are yellow things?" Ana asked, pointing to a cart piled high.

"Why, those are bananas," Rebecca said. "Haven't you ever eaten one?" Ana shook her head, but Rebecca didn't stop to explain. "There!" she exclaimed, pointing just ahead. "That man is selling sheet music." Rebecca stepped up to the tall cart, peering inside. "I'm looking for 'You're a Grand Old Flag,'" she told the peddler.

"Oy, such a little thing and already buying music," said the peddler, sifting quickly through the piles of colorful sheet music. "I'll bet you're playing the piano. In the tenements, they got practically nothing to eat, but a piano they got!"

Rebecca shook her head. "My teacher will play the piano. I'm going to sing in a school assembly." At least she hoped she was. Right now, she needed the words to the song to even have a chance.

The peddler pulled a red, white, and blue cover from deep under the jumbled pile. "The great music of George M. Cohan!" he bellowed. *"Mazel tov!* Congratulations! Today is your lucky day. A special price I'm giving on sheet music. So today you'll take this almost new copy for only ten cents."

"Ten cents?" Rebecca gulped. But she knew you never paid the asking price for anything on Orchard Street. She tried to remember how Bubbie got the peddlers to lower their prices. Bubbie argued and sometimes even insulted them, although nobody seemed to take it seriously.

"A robber!" Rebecca yelled. "A robber trying to trick a little girl!"

"Shah!" scolded the peddler. "You want to scare away all my customers?" He waved the sheet music just out of her reach. "Look at how perfect. Every page is here, and there isn't so much as a crease on the cover. So, I'll make you a bargain like you never heard. Take it home for just seven cents!"

"You think I'm a millionaire?" Rebecca asked, stalling for time. How could she get the man to lower the price again?

Ana's eyes were wide. "How much money do you have?" she whispered.

"Not that much!" Rebecca whispered back.

But the peddler heard every word, as if his hearing was tuned to the sound of every pigeon feather that dropped onto the sidewalk. "For such a talented singer, I'll give it away practically free for a nickel!"

Rebecca looked at the music. Here were the words she needed and the notes Miss Maloney could play on the piano in the assembly hall, if only she chose Rebecca to sing! She fingered the pennies in her pocket.

"There's a tear on the back cover," she said. "Two cents."

"You want my children should starve in the street?"

yelled the peddler. He put his hand over his heart, as if it were breaking.

If the peddler was going to be dramatic, Rebecca decided that might work for her, too. She pulled out her handkerchief and sniffled into it. "I can only spend three pennies," she whimpered, handing the music back. "Here, mister. I don't have to sing at the assembly." She looked up with sad eyes and started to leave. Ana patted her shoulder sympathetically, but as they walked away, Rebecca winked at her.

"Such children!" the peddler cried. "Like my own little girls. So you'll take it for three cents! This week I won't eat."

Rebecca beamed. She quickly handed over the pennies and took the sheet music. Then she steered Ana back to the banana peddler.

"I have here a young lady who has never eaten a banana," she said. "How many for one penny?" The man handed Rebecca two ripe bananas.

Ana spoke up. "That's all?" she asked, sounding insulted. "Only two for a whole penny?"

Rebecca stared in amazement. Her cousin really did catch on quickly.

The man handed her two green bananas. "Two for now, two for tomorrow," he said.

Rebecca paid her penny. She handed a ripe banana to her cousin, who promptly bit into the skin.

"No, no!" Rebecca cried. "Don't eat that." She peeled her banana to expose the fruit, and Ana did the same. "Now try it," Rebecca said.

Ana took a big bite. "Is wonderful," she said. "Fruit with its own wrapping! And I get four bananas for price of two."

Rebecca grinned. "That's what I call bargaining! Don't ever pay what they ask," she advised. "It's the first rule of living in New York."

"We play game with peddlers," Ana laughed. "We are smooth!"

# Two Songbirds

 ebecca had barely slept at all Monday night, going over the words to the song in her head. She didn't want to forget them in the middle of the audition! Tuesday morning she dressed quickly, eager to get to school. She tucked her doll into her pocket. "Wish me luck," she whispered to the wooden Beckie doll.

The morning routine was as hectic as it had been the day before. First Rebecca had to wait her turn to use the toilet in the hallway, then wait for a chance to wash at the sink, and finally wait for a chair to sit down for breakfast.

Papa and Uncle Jacob talked rapidly in Yiddish. "I went to all the builders, and none of them wanted a cabinetmaker. No one wants to hire a new immigrant," Uncle Jacob said. "One man told me to try the garment factories." He shrugged. "I suppose if I can cut a board, I can cut a piece of cloth."

"You don't want to work in a sweatshop," said Papa. "It's not healthy, and the pay is terrible." His forehead creased into a frown. "I wish the shoe store had more business. Then you could work with me."

"I know," Uncle Jacob said. "But you've done enough, Louis. I'm willing to take any job for a start."

As the girls headed off to school, Rebecca stopped in the entry to tuck the sheet music safely inside her coat. Pasta appeared from nowhere and rubbed against Rebecca's leg. She bent down to stroke the cat's fur, but it slipped out of reach and padded down to the basement. Outside, a cold drizzle fell, and the girls stepped up the pace.

"Today my papa is looking again for job," Ana said. "And your papa is going to Hebrew Immigrant Aid Society." Ana's face was pale. "I am afraid for my brother if infection on leg doesn't go away."

Rebecca couldn't think of anything to say. Ana was right—it made no sense that an injured leg could keep a boy out of the country. Besides, if Josef was too sick to stay in America, how could he go back to Russia alone?

Rebecca tried to take her mind off Josef by thinking about the audition. If just one of her classmates sang better than she did, Rebecca wouldn't be chosen to sing in the assembly.

As soon as the class had recited the Pledge of Allegiance, the students sat with their hands folded on their desks.

"We're going to start right off with the audition," Miss Maloney said. "We have very little time to prepare for this assembly, and I want it to go perfectly." She looked around the room. "Who would like to try a song?"

Five students raised their hands, including Rebecca. Two boys started off, and each one sang in a high, clear voice. But their songs had nothing to do with the flag or America. Rebecca was next.

Leo hid behind a book and stuck out his tongue at her. Rebecca turned her eyes away. She wasn't going to let Leo ruin her audition. She reached into her pocket and patted Beckie for luck. Then she sang out with a big smile. She imitated Max, giving the song rhythm. The other students began to clap along with her singing. Rebecca held her head high and marched in place.

When she got to the last words of the song—"Keep your eye on the grand old flag!"—she gave a sharp salute.

But Miss Maloney only said, "Thank you, Rebecca." Next, Sarah sailed through "The Star-Spangled Banner," but her ending was off-key. Finally, Lucy sang "Yankee Doodle Dandy." Rebecca's heart beat faster as Miss Maloney made her decision.

"I think you've all voted with your clapping," she said at last. "While each of our singers did well, I like the enthusiasm you showed for Rebecca's lively song. It seems just right for the assembly. It will be our grand finale!" Miss Maloney picked up a stack of papers. "Now I'll pass out some poems for you to learn. Since there are forty-two students in our class, each poem will be recited by two students together."

Rebecca squeezed her doll through her pocket and thought, *I'm going to sing for the entire school!* She pictured herself standing on the stage, singing along with the gay notes of the piano. She could almost hear the applause.

"Pay attention, Rebecca!" Miss Maloney was standing in front of her. Rebecca blinked as Miss Maloney repeated her words. "These poems are too hard for Ana, and I can't take a chance on anyone making mistakes at the assembly. Instead, I've decided to have her sing with you. I'm trusting you to teach her the song at home."

Rebecca was speechless. She had worked so hard for the chance to sing a solo, and now she would have to share it with her cousin. Immediately, she felt ashamed of her selfish thoughts.

Beside her, Ana opened the sheet music. "You're grend old fleg," she murmured.

*Why, Ana can barely pronounce the words!* thought Rebecca with alarm. Miss Maloney had said she couldn't take a chance on anyone making a mistake. What if Ana did? It would be so embarrassing!

Miss Maloney turned to write on the blackboard, and Lucy passed Rebecca a crumpled note. As Rebecca unfolded it, she glanced up. Lucy looked as if she was about to cry.

"No fair!" the note said. "Ana doesn't even know the song. She shouldn't get to sing."

*Lucy must feel terrible,* thought Rebecca. Lucy had auditioned, yet she wouldn't get to sing at all. Rebecca felt sorry for her friend, and she hoped Lucy wasn't blaming her. She stuffed the note into her pocket before Miss Maloney caught her.

Rebecca couldn't keep her mind on her work, and she was grateful when Miss Maloney took the class up on the roof for some exercise. The rain had stopped, and pale sunlight pushed through the clouds. Rose and several other girls surrounded Rebecca and Ana.

"You're so lucky," Rose said to Ana. "You've only been in school for two days, and now you're going to sing at the assembly!"

Ana clasped her hands together nervously. "I hope I can learn fastly," she said. She turned and smiled warmly at Rebecca. "But I not worry. My cousin will teach me."

Ana went off to try jumping rope with some of the girls, but Rebecca headed over to Lucy and Sarah. "I didn't ask Miss Maloney to let Ana sing," Rebecca explained. "It's not my fault."

"It's still not fair," Lucy said firmly. "She can barely speak English. How can she learn the song?"

"If she ruins the performance, the whole school will be laughing at us," Sarah added. "You're going to have to do a good job teaching her the song, or it *will* be your fault."

Rebecca's stomach tightened into a knot.

᠅

Rebecca was quiet on the way home, while Ana bubbled over with excitement. As they headed up the front stoop, Rebecca saw Mr. Rossi's curtains flap closed. Was he spying to see if Ana and her family had moved yet?

Ana raced up the steps, and in a stream of Yiddish, happily told Aunt Fannie and Mama about the assembly.

"Mazel tov! Congratulations!" said Aunt Fannie. She hugged Ana. "I'm so glad you are happy in the American school."

"We'd better practice," Rebecca said, "if you're going to learn the song." She took two apples from the bowl on the table. "Come on, Ana, I'll take you to the best place in the building." Ana followed Rebecca up the hall stairs, past Bubbie and Grandpa's apartment, all the way to the top of the stairway. Rebecca pushed open a rickety wooden door, and the girls stepped out onto the flat rooftop. There was a soft ruffling of feathers, and cooing sounds.

"Birds!" Ana exclaimed, rushing to the wire cages
stacked along one side of the roof.

"They're pigeons," Rebecca said. "They belong
to Mr. Rossi, but I like to come up and look at them.
I think they know me." She bit off a piece of her apple
and held it up to a cage. A tan bird with black spots on
its wings eagerly pecked at it. Rebecca reached in two
fingers and gently stroked its feathers.

"It's hard to imagine grouchy Mr. Rossi keeping
birds, isn't it," Rebecca said as the girls fed them pieces
of apple.

Ana nodded. When her apple was gone, she took
the sheet music from Rebecca. "I'm so glad we will sing
together at assembly," Ana said. "We will be two songbirds." She began to sing.

Rebecca listened as her cousin's melodic notes rose
above the cooing of the pigeons. At least Ana had a
pretty voice. If she could learn to pronounce the words
properly, she might make a good singing partner. If
not, the performance would be ruined.

Carefully, Rebecca had her cousin repeat the words.
"It's not 'grend,'" she explained patiently, "but 'grand.'

Listen to the a-a-a sound." Ana repeated the word until she got it right. Then they went on to the word "flag," and the same problem came back.

"No, no, no," Rebecca said, feeling exasperated. "It's fl-a-a-a-g, not fl-eh-g." But Ana couldn't seem to remember from one verse to the next. Over and over again, they sang the verses, but Ana either forgot the words or mispronounced them.

*If Ana can't sing the song properly,* Rebecca thought, *I'll be humiliated. And what's worse, my class will be embarrassed before the entire school.*

The wooden door creaked open, and Victor and Michael stepped out onto the roof.

"Beckie, Mama wants you girls to set the table," Victor said. "She's determined to get all thirteen of us in the parlor for dinner. Grandpa's bringing down more chairs."

"What have you heard about Josef?" Ana asked her brother, speaking in Yiddish.

Michael's slender body slouched against the wall. His short hair seemed as stiff as bristles on a new brush. "Josef is still sick with a fever from his infected leg. Doctors are treating him at the Ellis

Island infirmary, but they don't know if his leg will heal." Michael touched Ana's shoulder, and Rebecca saw that his hand was shaking. "If Josef loses his leg, he will have to go back to Russia."

"That would be so unfair," Rebecca said angrily. "Why does it matter if someone has an injured leg?"

"Papa told me that every immigrant has to be able to support himself," Victor explained. "A lame person can't work."

"That's ridiculous," Rebecca exclaimed. "Josef is only fifteen. His family will take care of him. Even if he is lame, he could be a lawyer or a bank clerk who sits at a desk all day!"

Victor shrugged. "Papa says it's the law."

"Well, it's a bad law," Rebecca declared.

Michael spoke up. "There's some good news, too. Papa found a job today, cutting cloth for coats."

Rebecca couldn't stop herself. "He's going to work in a sweatshop?" she blurted out.

Michael shrugged. "It's only until a better job comes along." He stood a little straighter. "I'm going to work, too. The dairy company needs boys to move the big milk cans from the delivery wagons to the warehouse.

Papa told the manager I was fourteen." He flexed his skinny arm. "The cans might be a bit heavy, but I will build up my muscles."

"What about school?" Rebecca asked.

"Since Josef isn't here, I must help earn money," Michael said. Then he looked a bit doubtful. "Maybe I can go to school at night—if I'm not too tired."

*Why are things going so wrong?* Rebecca asked herself. If Josef were sent back to Russia, his family would never see him again. Uncle Jacob had taken a job in a factory, where he would work long hours under terrible conditions. And now Michael had to leave school.

The rooftop door opened, and Mr. Rossi stood glaring at them. He held a pail of birdseed.

"This roof is not a playground. *Shoo!*" he called, as if they were birds who could fly away. Then Mr. Rossi realized exactly who was on the roof.

"You still here?" he asked Michael. "You can't stay any longer. I am telling landlord tomorrow."

"You don't need to tell the landlord anything, Mr. Rossi," Victor said. "My uncle just rented a tenement on Orchard Street. The whole family is going to move next week."

Fear filled Ana's eyes. "Orchard Street?" she echoed. "The place with dark buildings and big noises and—" Her voice broke as she turned to Rebecca. "I don't want to leave," she cried. "You are like sister to me." Rebecca reached out to hug her cousin, but Ana ran from the rooftop, leaving Rebecca and the cooing birds behind her.

"Now," Mr. Rossi said, "the rest of you, off the roof!"

# A New Flag Waves

hat night, Rebecca tried to comfort her cousin, but Ana's tears wouldn't stop. She cried herself to sleep, her handkerchief still clutched in her hand.

Rebecca tossed and turned, thinking about Ana moving to Orchard Street. Next week, Ana would go to a different school. Rebecca had expected her cousin to live with her for a long time and be her partner in everything. She remembered the excitement of bargaining with the peddlers, and thought about how much fun it was to dress alike. Just as Ana had said, they were like sisters. Even better—they were like twins.

It was wonderful having Ana with her all the time— at least, it was wonderful until Miss Maloney decided Ana should sing in the assembly. Now Rebecca's stomach twisted into knots whenever she thought about the performance. This was one thing she didn't want to do with Ana.

By morning, Rebecca was too tired to even talk, but it hardly mattered. Ana barely said a word all the way to school. Her eyes were puffy, and she seemed ready to cry again at any moment. Rebecca was silent, too, as the class filed into the big auditorium for rehearsal. The students lined up on the stage, facing the empty chairs where the rest of the school would sit in just two days.

"You may read your poems today, since it's just the first practice," Miss Maloney said. "But tomorrow is already Thursday, and you must have them memorized by then. Remember that this assembly is to show our respect for the flag. I expect each of you to recite your poems perfectly and with great feeling. Leo," Miss Maloney called, "you will begin the program by explaining why we have a new flag. Step forward, please."

Leo straightened his tweed jacket and puffed out his chest. "In 1912, America welcomed two new states to the Union," he began.

When Leo finished introducing the program, Lucy Valenti and Gertie Lowenstein read their poem.

"'Flag Song,' by Lydia Avery Coonley Ward," the girls said in unison.

> "Out on the breeze, o'er land and seas,
> A beautiful banner is streaming.
> Shining its stars, splendid its bars,
> Under the sunshine 'tis gleaming."

When they finished the last lines, two boys stepped forward. "'America for Me,' by Henry van Dyke," they announced.

All through rehearsal Rebecca fidgeted, anxiously awaiting her moment on the stage. She knew the song perfectly now. If only Ana would sing without any mistakes!

When all the other students had recited their pieces, Rebecca and Ana moved to the front of the stage. Miss Maloney sat down at the piano, spreading her silky black skirt across the piano stool. She opened the sheet music and played the opening notes. The girls began to sing.

Ana's rich voice sounded even prettier with the piano to accompany her. Rebecca tried to close her ears to her cousin's accent. Although Rebecca had drilled her repeatedly, Ana just couldn't seem to pronounce a short "a" sound. She said "fleg" instead of "flag" and "lend" instead of "land." As Rebecca boomed out the last two lines, she suddenly realized she was singing alone. Ana had forgotten the words completely! Ana looked at her in panic and then ran from the stage, her footsteps echoing down the hallway. Rebecca stood alone, her voice trailing off. Her classmates groaned.

"Let's be polite, children," Miss Maloney scolded them. "Rebecca and Ana are still learning the song."

*Me?* thought Rebecca. *Why, I know the song perfectly. It's Ana who's spoiling it!*

When the rehearsal was over, Rebecca found Ana alone in the classroom. As the other students filed in, Ana murmured, "I practice harder." She looked up at Rebecca. "You will help?"

Rebecca couldn't even answer. She took her pencil to the pencil sharpener, feeling the other students' eyes on her as she walked across the room.

Sarah cornered her. "Ana barely knows the words, and when she does, she can't even say them in proper English."

"Shhh," Rebecca said. "She might hear you." She

turned the pencil sharpener handle harder until the lead point was as sharp as a needle. "What can I do?" she demanded in a loud whisper. *"I'm* not the one making the mistakes!"

"Well, she's *your* cousin," Sarah said. She twisted a fold of her dress anxiously. "Please don't let her ruin the assembly. Our class will be the laughingstock of the school!" She put her hand on Rebecca's shoulder. "Why don't you just tell her she can't sing with you?"

Gertie chimed in from her seat nearby. "That would solve the whole problem. I'm sure Miss Maloney would agree. She said everything has to be perfect to show our respect for the flag."

Rebecca walked slowly back to her desk. Everyone was counting on her. *It will be my fault if the assembly is ruined,* she thought. Should she tell her cousin not to sing?

Then Rebecca thought of something else. Perhaps Ana didn't *want* to sing anymore. Now that she saw how difficult it was, she might be relieved if she didn't have to practice the words and worry about saying them perfectly. Next week, she would be going to a different school anyway, so maybe being part of the assembly didn't matter to her now.

When the class was dismissed for lunch, Ana stayed at her desk, hunched over the sheet music. Rebecca dawdled at the closet when she got her lunch box. *Maybe this is the time to tell Ana not to sing*, she thought. Then she heard her cousin's voice floating softly across the room. "You're grend old fleg and high-flyink fleg . . . " Rebecca grabbed her lunch box and hurried out to find Rose.

"Where's *En*na?" Otto Geller teased as Rebecca rushed by. "Is she looking at the *fleg?*"

Rebecca's face flushed with anger. She turned her back on Otto and marched over to join Rose.

"Everyone thinks it will be my fault if Ana ruins the assembly," Rebecca said to Rose as she sat down beside her.

Rose unwrapped a knish and took a bite of the potato-filled pastry. "What do *you* think?" she asked.

"I've tried to teach her the song, but there isn't enough time," Rebecca replied. "I think Ana might make a lot of mistakes."

"She might," Rose agreed. "It's very hard to learn English, and Ana's only been here a few days."

"If the assembly is ruined because of Ana, the whole class will be disappointed, including Miss Maloney. And I'll be the one who let them down. I bet no one will ever speak to me again."

Rose looked doubtful. "How long do you really think they'll remember?"

"Probably forever," said Rebecca. She still remembered her humiliation when Miss Maloney made her wear the dunce cap. But Rebecca suddenly realized that she hadn't thought about the dunce cap at all since that day. And none of her classmates had said a word about the dunce cap, not even Leo.

Rebecca nibbled at her lunch. "Sarah thinks I should tell Ana she can't sing with me. Maybe she's right. I'm sure Ana's worried about spoiling the song," Rebecca pointed out. "She must be worried, or she wouldn't have run off the stage this morning when she forgot the words. She might be relieved if I tell her not to sing."

"Maybe." Rose shrugged. "How would *you* feel if you were Ana?"

"Well, I know I wouldn't want to be embarrassed in front of the whole school," said Rebecca.

Miss Maloney rang the bell, and Rebecca followed Rose back to class. She had eaten only a few bites, but she didn't feel hungry at all.

Rose's question burned in her head for the rest of the day. *How would you feel?* Rebecca already knew how she'd feel if Ana *did* sing and made mistakes. But how would Ana feel if Rebecca kept her out of the assembly?

As soon as she opened her eyes Friday morning, Rebecca felt knots in the pit of her stomach. Yesterday's rehearsal had gone no better. Ana either forgot the words or pronounced them wrong. Miss Maloney had looked at the girls with pursed lips and hadn't said a word. Rebecca couldn't bear to let everyone down, especially her teacher.

Now the assembly was starting in just a few hours. If she was going to tell Ana not to sing, she had to do it soon. But Ana had already gone into the kitchen for breakfast. Quickly, Rebecca began getting dressed.

Rose's question pricked at her. *How would you feel if you were Ana?*

Well, how *would* she feel? Rebecca looked in the

mirror and pictured Ana saying to her, "Your voice not so pretty. I not want you to sing with me." Abruptly, Rebecca sat down hard on the bed as a hot wave of terrible feelings washed over her. She blinked, and then again she imagined it, Ana telling her not to sing. Again her chest burned with hurt and humiliation. The feeling was far, far worse than the embarrassment she had felt onstage when Ana forgot the words. Rebecca swallowed. Her mouth felt dry. She knew she would never forget it if Ana were to push her out of the assembly.

Mama beamed at the girls over breakfast. "It's so nice to see you matching every day." Rebecca managed a thin smile, but Ana didn't even look up.

Aunt Fannie handed each girl a small American flag. "We got these at Immigration when we came," she said. "Maybe they will bring you luck this morning when you sing."

Rebecca thanked her aunt politely and gave her flag a limp wave. Ana simply dropped hers into her pocket.

Bubbie came in with a plate of dark rolls, and Grandpa poked his head in the door. "I'll handle the store myself this morning," he said to Papa. "I hope everything goes well with Josef."

Papa, Aunt Fannie, and Uncle Jacob were going to Ellis Island once again. Josef's fever had broken, and the Hebrew Immigrant Aid Society had arranged for the family to meet with immigration officials. Rebecca's aunt had replaced her kerchief with one of Mama's hats, and Uncle Jacob had trimmed his beard neatly.

Suddenly Aunt Fannie sank into a chair. "What if the immigration men say Josef cannot stay?" she worried. "I could never forgive them."

It would be wrong to force Josef to leave America just because his leg wasn't perfect, Rebecca felt certain. Now she realized it would also be wrong to force Ana out of the assembly just because her English wasn't perfect. Maybe Rebecca and her classmates would be embarrassed if the song was a flop, but in just a few days, nobody would remember or care. Yet if she told Ana not to sing . . .

Rebecca ran to the bedroom and grabbed her doll from the pillow. *Please bring good luck today*, she whispered and slipped Beckie into her pocket.

As the girls headed down the street to school, Ana looked directly at Rebecca. "Don't worry," she said.

"I not sing today and ruin assembly."

Rebecca stopped still. "What do you mean? I didn't say anything about your singing." A shiver of shame crept up her neck. How could Ana have known what she had been thinking?

"You don't have to say anything to me," Ana said softly. "I hear you and Sarah and Lucy talking. You think I am dunce?"

Rebecca's heart sank. "I *was* worried about the performance," she admitted, "but now—now I *do* want you to sing with me, Ana. Honest."

"Now is too late," Ana said. "I tried hard, but I know things not always fair. Just like with Josef." She rushed ahead, leaving Rebecca to walk the rest of the way alone.

At school, Rebecca tried to talk to Ana as they filed into the auditorium. "We're two songbirds—remember?" But Ana turned away.

The class crowded together near the stage steps as Miss Maloney went to turn on the stage lights. Sarah pulled Rebecca aside.

"Did you tell her?" she whispered. Rebecca shook her head. Sarah didn't make a sound, but her mouth moved to form the words "Oh, no!"

Rebecca turned away, fighting back tears. Now *everyone* was unhappy with her. The performance hadn't even begun, and already she had ruined everything.

"Are we ready?" Miss Maloney said cheerily. "Line up, boys and girls."

As the students formed a line, Rebecca gazed at the high ceiling and the dark paneled walls. Painted in gold lettering along the top of the walls were the names of famous Americans: George Washington, Thomas Jefferson, Abraham Lincoln. She felt as if they were ready to welcome the new flag, too. But was she?

Rebecca took a deep breath and walked over to Ana. Her cousin had not joined the line of classmates waiting to step onto the stage. Rebecca pulled her Russian doll from her pocket. "You take Beckie," she said, handing the doll to Ana. "She brought me good luck in the audition, and now she'll bring us both good luck in the assembly."

Ana held the little doll close. "Do you really think I should sing, Rebecca?" she asked softly.

"Of course you should," Rebecca assured her.

"You have the prettiest voice in the class. Now come on, let's get in line!"

Feet shuffled and chairs creaked while the audience filed in to their seats. Then silence fell as Miss Maloney stepped to the front of the stage and welcomed the school to the assembly.

Leo began his opening speech, but Rebecca's heart was beating so loudly, she barely heard him. She looked out at the sea of upturned faces and drew in a shaky breath. There were so many people, all listening in complete silence. Would they notice every mistake? As her classmates recited their poems, Rebecca's hands began to tremble. It was almost time for her and Ana to sing.

At last, Miss Maloney played the lively opening notes on the piano, and the girls stepped forward. Together, they began the bouncy tune. Rebecca tried to smile and concentrate on her own singing. She barely noticed her cousin's accent and hoped the audience didn't notice it, either. Ana's strong voice lifted Rebecca's, and Rebecca's clear words carried Ana's. When they came to the last verse, Rebecca realized that the audience was clapping in rhythm and the assembly seemed alive with enthusiasm.

They had nearly made it to the end.

As the piano sounded its final chord, Ana suddenly pulled the small American flag from her pocket and waved it high. Surprised, Rebecca quickly did the same. The entire school cheered and applauded.

Then the lights dimmed, and a bright light shone on the new flag that hung from a pole at the side of the stage. Its rich colors stood out in the darkened hall. The audience rose, and everyone placed their right hands over their hearts and recited the Pledge of Allegiance. But Rebecca's ears were still ringing with the sound of applause. She and Ana had done it. They had sung for the whole school, and everything had been all right. Ana's accent hadn't mattered at all. And now Miss Maloney was beaming proudly as the principal came onstage and shook her hand. The assembly was a success.

Rebecca thought she saw tears brimming in Ana's eyes, but her cousin's face was lit up with happiness. Rebecca squeezed Ana's hand, and Ana squeezed back.

"Why did you wave your flag?" Rebecca whispered.

"I am feeling *patriotic*," Ana said, motioning to the back of the audience. "Look!"

Rebecca peered through the dim light and saw a row of people standing near the wall. She could see her mother, her father, Uncle Jacob, and Aunt Fannie—and beside them was a tall, lanky boy with a thickly bandaged leg, leaning on a wooden crutch. Rebecca waved her flag in his direction, and from his pocket, Josef pulled an identical flag and waved it high in the air.

# A Holiday Project

 few weeks after the school assembly, Rebecca sensed a sharp hint of snow in the air. She shivered with excitement. Winter was coming! That meant it was almost time for Hanukkah. And now that cousin Josef was safe with his family, Rebecca knew that this would be an extra special holiday season.

Rebecca and her friend Rose pushed against a biting wind as they made their way to school. Most of the shops were still closed, and the streets were quieter than usual. Not many people wanted to be out in such cold weather.

"I'm freezing," Rebecca said. She draped her scarf across her nose.

"I have goosebumples," Rose complained.

Rebecca giggled. "You mixed up two words, but

I like it. I have goosebumples, too."

All around, Rebecca saw Christmas decorations. "It seems like everything is red and green," she said to Rose. Store windows were framed in pine boughs, and some displayed miniature trees decorated with shiny glass balls and glittering ropes of tinsel. The doors on many of the row houses had pine wreaths with bright red ribbons. It seemed as if the entire neighborhood had changed from its drab everyday clothes into its best holiday outfit.

"I love seeing the candles in our *menorah*," Rebecca said, "but there really aren't any special decorations for Hanukkah, are there?"

"Sure there are," Rose replied with a sly smile. "We decorate our plates with *latkes*, and then we eat them!"

Rebecca could almost smell the crisply fried potato pancakes. "My mother's been buying potatoes by the bagful," she said. "We're going to make tons of latkes. Cousin Ana and her family are coming over on Friday night to celebrate the first night of Hanukkah. I can hardly wait!"

Best of all, Rebecca was going to wear her holiday dress. She had only worn it for Jewish New Year services in the fall, and then Mama had put it away to save for other special occasions. The dress had an overskirt with scalloped edges that made Rebecca feel as if she were wearing flower petals. It would be a Hanukkah treat just to wear it again.

When they arrived at the schoolyard, Rebecca and Rose hopped up and down, trying to stay warm. As soon as Miss Maloney rang her big brass bell, they hurried into the classroom. The radiators hissed, but the room was so cold that Rebecca hated to take off her coat and wool scarf. She rubbed her hands together briskly before she folded them on the desk in front of her.

"Let's warm up a bit," Miss Maloney said. "Stand up, everyone." She led the students as they stretched beside their desks, reaching high toward the ceiling. "Inhale," Miss Maloney said. As they bent over to touch their toes, she directed, "Exhale! Let's get our blood circulating." The room began to warm up, and a thin layer of moisture fogged the windows. The children took deep breaths in and out and moved their arms in little circles, but when Rebecca sat down again, her feet were still freezing.

Miss Maloney placed a wooden crate on her desk.

"Since it's almost Christmas," she said, "we are going to make a lovely gift for you to take home to your families." From the box she pulled a bright table decoration. A tall red candle rose from a base of greenery and berries. The fresh scent of pine wafted through the air.

"*Oooh!*" the students exclaimed in admiration.

"I made this centerpiece to show you what yours will look like," Miss Maloney explained. "I have collected all the materials we need." She pointed to the boughs that seemed to sprout from the base of the decoration. "The city allowed me to gather these fresh branches of balsam and pine in Central Park. The red berries came from wild rose bushes." Clusters of dried berries were nestled in the greenery, along with small pinecones. A vivid red bow added a cheerful finishing touch.

Rebecca gulped. They were going to make Christmas decorations! She glanced over at Rose, who wrinkled her forehead doubtfully.

"It's beautiful," sighed Lucy Valenti.

Miss Maloney pointed with pride to the tall red candle that stood in the center of the decoration. "These candles were generously donated to us by Mr. O'Hara at the candy store near my apartment.

Next week we will all write thank-you letters to him in our best handwriting, using pen and ink." Some of the boys groaned.

Rose raised her hand and stood stiffly by her desk when Miss Maloney called on her. "Excuse me," Rose said, "but at our house, we don't celebrate Christmas."

Miss Maloney smiled kindly, as if Rose simply didn't understand. "Christmas is a national holiday, children, celebrated by Americans all over the country. At the Capitol in Washington, D.C., there's even a decorated Christmas tree for everyone to enjoy."

Rose opened her mouth as if to argue, but then clamped it shut and sat down without another word.

The teacher set out round wooden disks to use as bases, along with pots of glue and pairs of scissors. She pulled baskets of green boughs from behind her desk and set out an assortment of pinecones, berries, and rolls of wide ribbon. She carefully unrolled a paper packet filled with candles.

"There are just enough candles for each of you to have one," she cautioned, "so work carefully. If you break your candle, it can't be replaced."

Rebecca wondered if it was true that the entire

country celebrated Christmas. Her family didn't. She looked around the room. Her friend Gertie Lowenstein was Jewish, and she was busily gathering greenery for her centerpiece. In fact, everyone in the class buzzed excitedly, except for Rose and Rebecca.

Miss Maloney handed Rebecca a wooden base and a red candle, and Rebecca took them reluctantly. Would it be wrong to do this school project? The other students had already set to work. And the centerpiece *was* beautiful. Rebecca hesitated for a moment, and then she had an idea about how to design hers.

She glued the candle carefully just off center. Then she selected several full branches to use around the base. She piled the boughs high and sniffed the piney scent that lingered on her fingers as she worked. The greenery smelled wonderful, almost spicy.

Yet an uneasy feeling nagged at her. She glanced over at Rose, who was frowning as she glued her candle to the base. Rose looked up and shrugged her shoulders, as if to say, *What can we do?*

Rebecca was still thinking about the project when

she walked home from school. Frozen grass crunched under her feet as she took a shortcut across Tompkins Square Park. Even though Rebecca saw Christmas decorations on many of the buildings, she knew that was just on the outside. Inside the row houses and tenements in her neighborhood, most of the families were getting ready to celebrate Hanukkah.

Was Miss Maloney right that Christmas was a national holiday? It was true that stores and offices in most parts of New York City were closed on December 25. But on the Lower East Side, where Rebecca lived, peddlers would be selling their wares from carts as they did every day, warming their hands over small coal stoves. The candy store, the fish shop, and the delicatessen would be open as usual. Papa and Grandpa would go to work at the shoe store.

As she walked down the street to her own building, Rebecca looked up to see Hanukkah menorahs standing in many windows. The nine-branched candelabras were of different designs in gleaming silver or golden brass. Miss Maloney's greenery and red candles just wouldn't seem right in Jewish homes.

Rebecca was so lost in thought that she nearly

bumped into Mr. Rossi, who was sniffling as he swept the front steps.

"*Aah-choo!*" he sneezed, pulling a handkerchief from his pocket. He blew his nose with a noisy *honk!*

"Bless you," Rebecca said politely.

Mr. Rossi only grumbled. "I'm feeling sicker by the minute. I gotta get to bed." He frowned up at the dark clouds overhead. "How can I shovel these steps if it snows? How am I gonna take care of the birds?" His eyes were red and watery. "And now the cat is gone. She'll freeze if she's lost outside. I can't go looking for her and maybe get sicker."

Rebecca was always amazed that grouchy old Mr. Rossi looked after Pasta, the cat, and kept gentle pigeons in cages on the roof of the building. She went up to the rooftop often to talk to the birds and stroke their soft feathers. But Mr. Rossi chased the children away if he caught them on the roof.

"I'll keep an eye out for Pasta," Rebecca said. "And you shouldn't go out on the roof if you're sick. Maybe I could feed the pigeons for you." Mr. Rossi couldn't shoo her off if she was helping him!

The janitor turned away with a fit of coughing,

dragging the broom down the steps to his basement apartment. Rebecca noticed that his window was dark, and there were no holiday decorations anywhere, not even a paper snowflake. Just before he opened his door, he muttered, "If you're feeding my birds, you gotta be here before supper. Those birds need to eat to stay warm."

Rebecca skipped up the stairs and searched the hallway on each landing, but there was no sign of Pasta. The cat could be as cranky as Mr. Rossi, but Rebecca loved the pigeons—and now she was going to take care of them herself.

Inside the warm kitchen, Sadie was polishing the family's Hanukkah menorah. Sophie stood by holding a dish towel.

"Mr. Rossi's sick, so I'm going to take care of his pigeons," Rebecca exclaimed. "I am filled with unbounded joy."

"You're filled with *what?*" Sadie asked.

"Unbounded joy," Rebecca repeated. "That's how the Rebecca in this story feels when something won-derful happens." She held up her latest book, *Rebecca of Sunnybrook Farm*. It was the best book she had ever checked out of the library. She had read dozens of books, but none of the characters was as interesting as Rebecca Randall.

Sophie buffed the menorah until it gleamed and then set it on the windowsill in the parlor. Sadie put two candles in their proper places.

"I suppose you'll also be filled with joy when you light the Hanukkah candles. You're still not old enough to light the Sabbath candles," Sadie taunted, "but even little Benny gets to light candles for Hanukkah." She whispered something to Sophie, and the twins went off to the bedroom and closed the door.

Rebecca bristled. She hated the way her sisters acted so grown-up all the time. Just because they were allowed to light the Sabbath candles every Friday night, they treated her like a baby. Rebecca hoped Mama would let her light candles someday soon. She dreamed of having candlesticks of her own and standing beside her sisters to light Sabbath candles, too.

Happily, Hanukkah was one holiday when even the youngest in the family had a turn to kindle the lights. The menorah held nine colorful wax candles—one for each of the eight nights of the holiday and a head

candle, called the *shammas*, that was used to light the
others. On the first night, Papa lit the shammas, and
the youngest child held it to the wick of the first candle.
That was always Benny's turn. Then each night of Hanukkah, one additional candle was added to the menorah, and Rebecca always had the second turn. Every
night of the holiday, they added one more candle until
all nine burned brightly. Rebecca loved the flickering
Hanukkah lights that seemed to melt away the winter
darkness, if only for a week.

Mama came into the kitchen lugging a bag of potatoes. "I think that's finally enough!" she declared, pour-
ing the potatoes into a wooden bin near the doorway.

Rebecca started to tell her about the centerpiece.
Mama would know if it was the right thing to do.
"Today in school we started a project," she began.
"Do you think it's all right if—"

"Oy, such a load!" exclaimed Bubbie. She set a
bulging oilcloth bag filled with potatoes on the work
shelf of the tall kitchen cabinet.

Rebecca decided to wait and talk to Mama after
Bubbie went upstairs to her own apartment. She didn't
want to mention the centerpiece in front of Bubbie until

she knew whether Mama would approve. Instead, Rebecca bundled into her coat and scarf.

"I'm going out to feed the pigeons for Mr. Rossi," she announced. "He's got a bad cold." Then she remembered the lost cat. "Have you seen Pasta around? Mr. Rossi thinks she's lost."

"That messy cat," Bubbie said. "Always under my feet on the stairs. Good riddance!"

Rebecca dashed out the front door of the building and down the steps. She knocked lightly at Mr. Rossi's door, which had its own entrance. When there was no answer, she rapped harder. After what seemed like forever, he opened the door a crack.

"I think you not coming. Kids today is so lazy. Here," he said, handing Rebecca two small pails. "Fill one dish in every cage with water, one with seeds." Then he handed her a damp rag. "You gotta clean out the dishes first." Rebecca tried to smile at him, but Mr. Rossi had already shut the door. He didn't like children, Rebecca knew. He especially didn't seem to like her.

The birds cooed and flapped in their cages when Rebecca approached, as if they knew it was time to eat.

One pair of birds lived in each cage. Mr. Rossi had built a slanted roof over the cages for the winter. Rebecca thought the pigeons looked nice and cozy in their sheltered home.

She looked out at the rooftops that stretched across the neighborhood as far as she could see. None of them had pigeon cages. The gentle birds living on her rooftop made Rebecca feel that there wasn't another building in New York that was as special as hers.

She opened each cage, cleaned and filled the seed and water dishes, and made sure the latches were secure. The pigeons dipped their beaks into the water dishes and pecked eagerly at the seeds. As Rebecca watched them, a large white pigeon sailed onto the roof above the cages.

"Where did you come from?" Rebecca asked softly. She put a few seeds into her hand, and the bird pecked at them. "Oh, you're hungry, are you?" Rebecca giggled as its beak tickled her palm.

Was this a wild bird that had come for a handout, or had one of Mr. Rossi's birds escaped? She had noticed that one cage was empty. Rebecca placed a small pile of seeds at the bird's feet and hurried down the stairs.

As she passed the door that led to the basement, she heard a strange mewling sound. The door was open, and the steep wooden stairs were dark. Rebecca stopped and heard the faint sound again. Maybe Pasta had chased after a mouse and had gotten hurt. She stepped down the rickety stairway and tried to see in the dim light. Pieces of coal littered the floor, and dirty buckets were strewn about. Only Mr. Rossi came down here, when the furnace needed more coal.

Rebecca saw a slight movement against one wall. She could barely make out a heap of rags and a shadowy shape on top. Then she heard a soft mew. It was Pasta! Rebecca picked her way down the steps and inched closer. As she reached down to pick up the lost cat, Pasta hissed at her. Rebecca jumped back, but not before she saw two tiny kittens nuzzling their mother for milk. Pasta's eyes were wide, but the kittens' eyes were shut tight.

"No wonder you don't want me to get too close," Rebecca said softly. "Don't worry, Pasta, I'll help you take good care of your babies."

"Mr. Rossi!" she called as she approached his apartment. She banged on the door.

"So, you have trouble already, eh?" the old man wheezed.

"Oh, no," Rebecca said. "No trouble at all. And I found Pasta. She's in the basement with two new kittens. They're so tiny! Wait till you see them."

"Work, work, work," Mr. Rossi complained. "And more mouths to feed!"

"There's other news, too. While I was feeding the birds, a big white pigeon landed on the roof, and I was afraid one of your birds had gotten loose."

Mr. Rossi's face brightened. "A white pigeon?" he asked. "Open the empty cage for it. But first take the message."

"Message?" Rebecca asked. "The bird can't talk!"

"Maybe not," he said mysteriously, "but it can bring news." He looked at Rebecca doubtfully. "You don't see a little tube on its leg? Inside is a note. Open the tube and bring the message to me, yes?"

Rebecca bounded up the stairs, nearly crashing into Bubbie as her grandmother headed upstairs.

"What?" Bubbie exclaimed, moving out of the way. "This is a race you're in?"

But Rebecca just yelled, "Sorry! I have to catch a

bird!" She opened the creaky roof door slowly, so that she wouldn't frighten the new pigeon away. It was still standing on the rooftop, cocking its head in her direction. Rebecca approached cautiously, but it didn't seem to mind when she picked it up and pried open the slender tube that was attached to its leg.

"Oh, you *do* have a secret message!" she cried, gently removing a tightly rolled paper. She wanted to know what it said, but that would be like reading Mr. Rossi's mail. After all, it wasn't a message for her. She pocketed the rolled note and opened the door of the empty cage. Without any coaxing, the white pigeon fluttered in.

Questions flooded into Rebecca's mind as she filled the bird's dishes. Where had the white pigeon come from? How had it found her building? And what did the message say?

Rebecca was sure Mr. Rossi had the answers, but he might think she was being nosy and get angry with her if she asked. She hurried back down the steps to his apartment. When Mr. Rossi opened his door, Rebecca hesitated, gathering her courage. Just as she handed him the thin paper and opened her mouth to speak, Mr. Rossi pointed to a dish of milk. "Now you gotta feed Pasta, too." Then he started coughing. He waved Rebecca away and closed the door with a firm *click*.

# A Secret Shared

ebecca couldn't wait to tell her sisters about the kittens and the mysterious white pigeon, but when she headed to the bedroom, there was a sign on the closed door: *"Keep Out!"*

"Let me in," Rebecca demanded, giving the door a kick. "This is my room, too!"

Sadie came to the door and opened it no wider than Mr. Rossi had opened his. "You can come in, I guess," she whispered. "But be quiet!"

Sophie was sitting on her bed, hiding something behind her back.

"What are you doing?" Rebecca asked. Her sisters looked at each other.

"Go ahead and tell her," Sophie said.

But Sadie hesitated. "Can you keep a secret?"

"Of course I can," Rebecca said.

"Do you absolutely, positively promise not to breathe a word of what we're doing?" Sadie demanded.

Rebecca plunked herself down on her sisters' bed and crossed her arms across her chest. "I don't care if you tell me or not! I have secrets of my own."

Sophie carefully pulled out a long table scarf embroidered with gay flowers. "I'm sewing this for Bubbie," she whispered. "We've been making Hanukkah gifts to surprise everyone."

"You made something for everyone?" Rebecca asked, impressed.

"Well, not yet," said Sadie.

Sophie added, "We're running out of time."

Rebecca picked up one end of the table scarf. "Bubbie will love this. She can put it in her parlor. Do you have something for Grandpa?"

Sadie shook her head, and the tight curl at her forehead bobbed. "We're stumped on what to make for him," she admitted. "Any ideas?"

Rebecca thought for a moment. Grandpa wore a prayer cap on his head all the time, even under his hat when he went out. "He might like a new *yarmulke*," she suggested. Then her face lit up. "Maybe I could crochet one for him. I have some silvery gray thread."

"It would match his hair," Sadie quipped. The three girls giggled together.

"All right," Sadie decided. "You can help. Just remember—it's our secret! Now, what's yours?"

Rebecca sat up straighter, delighted that her sisters were including her in their holiday plan. For once, they weren't treating her like a baby. She pulled out her crochet bag and chose a hook. "Guess what? Pasta had kittens! They're in the basement, and their eyes are still shut. They must have just been born. I got to bring Pasta a dish of milk."

"I can't wait to see them," Sadie said. "They're like a Christmas present for Mr. Rossi."

Rebecca laughed. "I don't think he's too happy about having more cats, but he was excited about something else. He got a secret message today," she announced with an air of importance. "It came by *pigeon!*"

"Really?" Sophie asked, her eyebrows lifting in surprise. "I didn't know Mr. Rossi's birds were homing pigeons. I read in my history book that when Napoleon lost the battle of Waterloo, a carrier pigeon brought the news to France four days faster than a soldier on horseback."

"Maybe the message is about the war in Europe," Sadie exclaimed. "What did it say?"

"I don't know yet," Rebecca said, looping stitches with the crochet hook. "After all, it was a secret. I'm going to try to get Mr. Rossi to tell me tomorrow."

But she wasn't sure how. *What would Rebecca of Sunnybrook Farm do?* She was pretty sure *that* Rebecca wouldn't lose her courage at the last moment. *Maybe if I just ask him, he'll tell me everything!* But Mr. Rossi would have to open his door more than a crack.

A knock sounded on the bedroom door, and the girls froze. "Don't come in!" they squealed.

"Supper!" Mama called. "Whatever you three are up to, it's going to have to wait."

Rebecca started singing as she walked into the kitchen. "Jingle bells, jingle bells . . ." She had just reached the part about dashing through the snow when Bubbie swooped into the kitchen.

"What you are singing?" she demanded.

Rebecca stopped in mid-verse. "It's a song we sing in school," she said. Why was Bubbie upset?

"This song is for Christmas, not for you!" Bubbie
chided her.

"But it's just about riding through snow on a
sleigh," Rebecca protested. "You told me you loved
sleigh rides when you were a girl in Russia."

"Never mind about Russia!" Bubbie said sternly.
"No more of this Christmas singing."

Mama pulled a steaming noodle casserole from
the oven. The kitchen filled with the scent of cheese
and a hint of cinnamon. "Christmas is all around us,
I'm afraid," said Mama. "It seems there are more decorations in the city every year."

"It's all over the neighborhood yet!" Bubbie complained, cutting big squares of the noodle *kugel*. "The
shop windows have little trees with colored balls hanging, and everywhere are these round things—reefs!"
She made a big circle with her hand, and sputtered,
"Can you believe it? There's even one hanging from
the bagel man's cart on Orchard Street!"

"Ahh," Mama nodded as they all sat down at the
table. "*Wreaths*. That lovely greenery, and the pretty
bows."

In her excitement about the kittens and the white

pigeon, Rebecca had nearly forgotten about her school project. If Bubbie didn't want her to sing "Jingle Bells," she would surely be angry if she found out Rebecca was making a centerpiece with greenery and a red bow! But Mama had said the wreaths were lovely. Maybe *she* would like the decoration.

Benny waited as Papa cut a square of kugel into bite-sized pieces for him. "Papa, did you hang a reef at the shoe store?"

Papa fidgeted with his tie. "No, not a wreath," he said slowly.

"Then *what*?" Benny insisted. He speared a noodle with his fork.

"Well, just a few green boughs." Papa looked sheepishly at Bubbie, who was frowning. "We have to make the window look festive," he explained, "like the other stores."

*Maybe Papa could put my centerpiece in the store,* Rebecca thought. But as she looked at Bubbie's scowling face, she felt sure her grandmother wouldn't approve.

Rebecca looked around the table uncertainly. "Miss Maloney says Christmas is an American holiday—for everyone to celebrate," she said.

*"Phooey!"* Grandpa declared, slicing a loaf of thick black bread. "Christmas is a Christian holiday. We are Jewish, so we don't celebrate it, no matter how American we are."

Rebecca was silent. If Grandpa learned of the school project, he would be as upset as Bubbie.

"Our friends at school say Hanukkah isn't a very important holiday for Jews, but Christmas is the most important holiday for Christians," Sadie put in. "The students who celebrate Christmas get gifts, and some of our Jewish friends do, too!"

"We already have the very best gift of all," Papa said firmly. "In America we have the gift of being free to celebrate our own holiday."

No one else said a word, but Rebecca and her sisters exchanged knowing looks. Every year, Grandpa gave each of the children a shiny half-dollar. The money was called Hanukkah *gelt* in Yiddish, and it carried on an old tradition. Rebecca loved the feel of the heavy silver coin, and the money would last her for a long time. But when it came to presents, this year was going to be different. Everyone would receive a gift, not just the children. Wouldn't Papa be surprised!

After the dishes were cleared away, the twins went off to their room together, but now Rebecca didn't mind. She knew they weren't leaving her out. She would work on Grandpa's yarmulke before she went to bed. How exciting it was to share a secret with her sisters!

Victor settled at the kitchen table to do his homework, complaining about how many arithmetic problems he had to work out.

"Here is a problem for you to figure," Grandpa said with a sparkle in his eyes. "There are eight nights of Hanukkah, and we light one additional candle each night. Every night the candles burn all the way down, and the next night we start with new ones. So, how many candles do we need to last the whole week?" Victor's eyes narrowed with concentration. "I give a little hint," Grandpa added. "Don't forget to count the extra shammas each night!"

As Victor started writing down a long column of numbers, Rebecca leaned toward Grandpa and whispered, "Forty-four!" It was just loud enough for her brother to hear.

Victor glared at her. "You already knew the answer!" he accused her. "No one could figure it out that fast."

"I can," Rebecca declared. "I'm used to Miss Maloney's arithmetic teasers. We figure out problems in our head in no time." She went into the parlor and pulled a chair closer to the fireplace so that she'd be warm while she read her library book.

"Such a fine mathematics student you are," Grandpa said, pulling up a chair beside her. "There is a word I hear for this . . ." He thought for a moment, trying to remember. "Whiz!" he grinned. "You are arithmetic whiz!"

"Then let her do my homework!" Victor called from the kitchen.

Mama switched on the parlor lamp. A soft glow fell across Rebecca's book.

Grandpa opened his Yiddish newspaper. "So, what your book is about?"

"It's the best book," Rebecca said, "but there are some parts that I don't quite understand. Listen to this." She read aloud to Grandpa. "'The traits of unknown forebears had been wrought into her fibre.' What do you suppose that means?"

Grandpa rubbed his beard. "Maybe if it was in Yiddish, I could help you."

Rebecca looked down at the book and then back at Grandpa. "Mostly, the story is about a girl named Rebecca who lives with two aunts she barely knows, just so she can go to school," Rebecca said. She couldn't imagine leaving her family and living with strangers. "Rebecca's so brave. I don't think I could do that."

Grandpa patted her hand. "Courage comes when you need it," he said, speaking in Yiddish, as he often did. "I didn't think I could leave Russia and come to America. It was hard, starting all over again and not speaking one word of English!"

"That took real courage," Rebecca agreed. Her cousin Ana had done that, and Rose, too. Maybe that was why Rose had been brave enough to tell Miss Maloney she didn't want to make the centerpiece. Standing up to a teacher wasn't nearly as hard as moving to a new country. Still, Rebecca knew she didn't even have the nerve to question Miss Maloney about the assignment.

She looked over at Grandpa as he read his newspaper. "Miss Maloney thinks Christmas is so important that we should all put up decorations to celebrate," Rebecca said quietly.

Grandpa shook his head and made a *tsk-tsk* sound with his tongue. Rebecca felt a flutter of guilt. It was as if Grandpa had declared, "You must not make the centerpiece!"

Rebecca glanced toward the family's menorah gleaming on the windowsill. The tinted candles stood tall, waiting for the first night of Hanukkah. "Grandpa, is it true that Hanukkah isn't really a very important Jewish holiday?" she asked.

Grandpa folded his newspaper onto his lap. "Long ago," he began, "the Jews were ruled by a king who prayed to statues of different gods. The king decreed that all his subjects must worship as he did. His soldiers rampaged through the temple where the Jews prayed and smashed everything they could. It was a frightening time. Many Jews were afraid to disobey the king's law. Others just wanted to fit in, to be like everyone else."

"Miss Maloney thinks everyone should dress and speak the same," Rebecca said. "And especially, no talking in Yiddish!"

"Immigrants have to learn new ways to live here in America," Grandpa admitted. "But we can't forget who we are, even if it means being a little different."

Rebecca felt a wave of understanding. "Wait a minute—that's what the sentence in my book is about!" she exclaimed.

Grandpa looked puzzled, and now it was Rebecca's turn to explain. "When it says that 'the traits of unknown forebears were wrought into her fibre,' I think it's just a fancy way of saying that the habits that made Rebecca different from other people were passed down from her ancestors. That makes her special. Do you think the Jews felt like that, long ago?"

"Absolutely!" Grandpa said. "Many of them refused to give up their religion, even for the king. One brave group fought the king's entire army—and they won. If they hadn't, there wouldn't be any Jews left today. That's part of what we celebrate every year on Hanukkah." Grandpa reached over and tapped Rebecca on her head. "Do you think that's important?" Rebecca nodded solemnly.

Grandpa pointed to the menorah. "Remember why we light the candles for eight nights?" He didn't wait for Rebecca to answer. "When the Jews cleaned their temple, they wanted to re-light the special lamp that stood near the altar. But they could find just one small vial of sacred oil to place in the lamp. It was only enough to last for one day, but that little bit of oil burned for eight full days. Many thought it was a miracle, to show them they had done the right thing in fighting against the king."

"In my book, Rebecca Randall always does what she thinks is right," Rebecca told Grandpa, "even if grown-ups sometimes get angry."

"A girl with *chutzpah*," Grandpa said.

Rebecca thought about the school project again. Maybe she needed a little chutzpah, too. Maybe she should be brave enough to tell Miss Maloney she wouldn't make the centerpiece.

As Grandpa adjusted his prayer cap, Rebecca remembered she still needed to work on his present. She stood up and faked a yawn. "Well, I'm going off to bed," she fibbed.

Bubbie looked up from her crocheting. "What, so early?" she asked. "You hardly read two pages! You feel sick, maybe?"

"No, I'm just really tired," Rebecca pretended, and slipped into her room. The twins were busily working. Rebecca could hardly believe they were letting her be part of their plan. It was as though she had just tasted something new and delicious. For now, she could forget her worries about school and the centerpiece and simply enjoy sharing a secret with her sisters. Round and round she crocheted the prayer cap for Grandpa, until it grew big enough to fit on his head. She finished it off with two white stripes around the edge and held it up proudly.

Sadie patted her shoulder. "You actually made a yarmulke!" she said. "It's beautiful. How about another one for Papa?"

Rebecca nodded with enthusiasm. This year, when her parents gave out Hanukkah gelt, she and her sisters would have something to give them in return.

"This is going to be the best Hanukkah ever," Rebecca whispered as she reached for a new ball of thread.

# Minding
# Miss Maloney

 can't wait to wear my holiday dress,"
Rebecca said the next morning. "It's
almost spandy new."

Mama blinked in surprise. "I suppose that's
Rebecca of Sunnybrook Farm talking again," she
laughed. "Ever since you started reading that book, I
feel as if I have four daughters instead of three!" She
put a plate of breakfast rolls on the table. "Your dress
may be spandy new, but you are a lot taller than you
were a few months ago. I'm sure the sleeves and the
hem need to be let down a few inches. I have so much
cooking to do, I'll never have a chance to sew it before
tomorrow night, when Hanukkah begins. You'll just
have to wear a school dress."

Rebecca's heart sank. "But Mama," she argued, "with
company coming I wanted to wear my holiday dress!"

The twins came in for breakfast. "You should have thought of that before you grew," Sadie teased. "Did you think your dress would grow along with you?" Sophie smiled at the joke. As they sat down, there was a musical tinkling sound.

"I hear bells!" Benny cried in astonishment. He tilted his head back to look up at Sadie and Sophie. "It's you!" he laughed, pleased that he had solved the mystery.

The twins had tied long red ribbons in their hair, and a small metal bell dangled at the end of each streamer. Every time they moved, the bells gave a merry jingle. Benny reached up, trying to shake them.

Mama's lips pursed into a thin line. "You can take those ribbons off right now," she said.

"But Mama, they're just for fun!" Sadie protested.

"All the girls are wearing them," Sophie added.

"Well, I know two girls who are not," Mama said firmly. "You're going to school to study, not to be in a costume play!" She held out her hand with the palm up, waiting.

"Oh, Mama," the twins whined.

"You will not leave the house with such silliness,"

Mama said. "I can just imagine what Bubbie would say if she saw you!"

With a pout, the twins untied the ribbons and handed them over. As Rebecca brushed past her sisters to get her coat, she leaned toward them and hummed a few bars of "Jingle Bells" so softly that only they heard. Their faces flushed with anger. Giggling, Rebecca grabbed her coat and ducked out the door before they could catch her.

On the way out, Rebecca stopped to visit the new kittens. They were sleeping soundly, and Pasta watched them protectively. Rebecca didn't try to touch them— not yet. There would be plenty of time to play with them when they grew bigger.

Rose was waiting outside for Rebecca. "I like the lions carved on each side of your row house door," Rose said as the girls fell into step together. "Otherwise, your building looks like every other one on the street."

It was true. Each brick row house had a tall front stoop, four floors, and large windows spaced evenly apart. "On the outside, the buildings do look pretty much the same," Rebecca agreed, "but my building is different in another way, too."

"What's different about it besides the lions?" Rose asked.

"Pigeons!" Rebecca exclaimed as they turned the corner. "Mr. Rossi, our janitor, keeps pigeons on the roof. He uses them to send messages!"

"They must be homing pigeons," Rose said, her eyes wide. "What are the messages about?"

"I tried to ask him yesterday, after I fed the birds," Rebecca said, "but he's so grumpy. Before I could say a word, he shut his door right in my face! He doesn't like anyone—especially kids. He's always complaining when we play in front of the building." She waved her hand, as if dismissing Mr. Rossi. "Well, I don't like *him* very much, either—just his pigeons. And now his cat has kittens. So I guess I should feel lucky he lives in our building." The two girls hurried on to school, their arms linked together.

When class began that morning, Miss Maloney was in a festive mood. Instead of singing "The Star-Spangled Banner" to start the day, she had the class sing one of the carols they had learned. Everyone stood and sang "Hark! The Herald Angels Sing." Rebecca loved singing, and the melody was beautiful, but as she came to the last lines, she fell silent. "With the angelic host proclaim, Christ is born in Bethlehem," sang the other students. Rebecca wasn't sure what an angelic host was, but she *was* sure that if Bubbie had scolded her for singing "Jingle Bells," she would be furious if she found out Rebecca was singing this.

"As my Christmas present to each of you," Miss Maloney said when they finished, "there will be no penmanship exercises and no arithmetic lesson today." The class erupted in cheers. "Instead, we will spend the entire morning working on our centerpieces."

The students crowded to the back of the room, where their unfinished decorations were lined up. Rebecca found hers without even checking for her name on the bottom. It was the one with the candle set to the side and the greenery piled extra high. She held it one way, and then turned it another. In spite of her misgivings, she couldn't help admiring the effect. After all, it was just a decoration. How could making something so pretty be wrong? She would try not to think about what to do with it until she was done.

"Work quickly, children," Miss Maloney said.

"The glue must be dry by tomorrow so that you can take your projects home."

Tomorrow! Rebecca hadn't known she would have to take her project home so soon! She remembered Mama's displeasure with the twins for wearing red ribbons and bells. And Bubbie didn't like to hear or see anything that smacked of Christmas. Rebecca swallowed hard, and a taste like sour lemons washed down her throat. She couldn't take a Christmas decoration home, no matter how pretty it was.

Miss Maloney had said there were no extra candles. *If my candle broke, I wouldn't be able to finish my decoration,* she thought. The bright red candle seemed like a lighthouse ready to shine its beacon across a sea of greens. It would be wasteful to spoil it, but she saw no other way to get out of the project. Taking a deep breath, she turned the centerpiece upside down and gave it a shake. A few pine needles dropped from the rustling branches, but the candle didn't budge. Rebecca had glued it down firmly. She let out a deep sigh and turned it right side up again.

"Mother is going to love my decoration," Gertie declared. "She's already put balsam around the windows.

I think she'll want this on the mantel, over the tinsel cord."

"You put up Christmas decorations?" Rebecca asked. "But you're Jewish!"

"We don't *celebrate* Christmas," said Gertie. "We just like the decorations. As Miss Maloney says, it's an American holiday."

Rebecca had heard that some Jewish families had Christmas decorations, but she had never actually known anyone who did. Her family would never agree with Gertie's, she was certain. She set her unfinished centerpiece on her desk and poked at the spiky pine branches.

"Isn't it fun making this centerpiece?" Lucy grinned. "It's so much better than practicing handwriting!"

"That's true," Rebecca agreed. "But then, your family celebrates Christmas, so they'll enjoy the decoration." Very softly she added, "I don't know what I'm going to do with mine." She followed Lucy to Miss Maloney's desk and gathered up handfuls of berries and pinecones.

"Aren't you going to give it to your mother?" Lucy asked with surprise.

Rebecca shook her head. The centerpiece could never be a Hanukkah gift. "We don't have decorations," she explained. "We celebrate a different holiday called Hanukkah."

"Then you don't even have a Christmas tree?" Lucy asked.

Rebecca shook her head. "Nope."

Lucy put her arm around Rebecca. "That's too bad," she said.

"No, it isn't," Rebecca said. "Our whole family is getting together and we're going to have a real feast. Every night we sing songs and play a game called *dreidel*."

Lucy looked puzzled. "On Christmas, we celebrate the birth of baby Jesus," she said. "We put up beautiful decorations to make everything sparkle, even in the middle of winter. What does Hanukkah celebrate?"

Rebecca remembered what Grandpa had told her. "Hanukkah is also called the Festival of Lights, because we light special candles every night. That's to remember how Jewish people long ago fought a king's army so that they could worship in their own temple." Rebecca's excitement about Hanukkah bubbled out of her. "It's my absolute favorite holiday of all, and it lasts a whole week!"

"But there's nothing wrong with you making this centerpiece, is there?" Lucy asked.

"I don't know," Rebecca admitted.

Miss Maloney's pinched voice caught Rebecca's ear, and she turned away from Lucy. "Oh, dear me," Miss Maloney was saying to Rose. "You don't want all your pinecones jumbled in one place!" Rebecca watched Miss Maloney snap off several of the tiny pinecones. "You must balance the decorations around the entire centerpiece," she instructed. Globs of white glue stuck to the branches where Miss Maloney had removed pinecones, and Rose's candle tilted crookedly.

"I don't care what it looks like," Rose muttered to Rebecca under her breath.

Back at her desk, Rebecca began nestling berries and pinecones together on the pine boughs. Each time she bent over the fragrant greenery, she imagined she was deep in a pine forest. She stepped back and looked at what she had accomplished so far. It was such a beautiful decoration. If only it weren't for Christmas!

Miss Maloney stopped at Rebecca's desk. "How

lovely!" she exclaimed. "Rebecca, I believe you have an artistic flair!" She held the centerpiece up. "Look, everyone," she said, "this design is a bit different. The greenery is so full, and the pinecones and berries are placed together beautifully. Good job."

Rebecca thought this should be another moment of unbounded joy. Miss Maloney had praised her work out of all the projects in the class. If only it had been a page of perfect arithmetic problems instead of this!

"What are you going to do with your centerpiece tomorrow?" Rebecca asked Rose as they walked home. The air was so cold that it seemed as if her words froze as she spoke.

Rose didn't hesitate. "Throw it away."

"How could you throw away something so pretty?" Rebecca asked. "And it has a spandy new candle in it, too!"

Rose could barely shrug through her heavy coat and scarf, but Rebecca saw the familiar gesture. "Miss Maloney says to make it, so I do. My mother won't have Christmas decorations in the house, so I'll toss it in the trash before she ever sees it. What are you going to do with yours?"

Rebecca copied Rose's shrug, but she didn't have an answer. How could she give Grandpa a prayer cap and at the same time bring home a Christmas decoration? Grandpa would be so disappointed in her after all he had explained about the importance of Hanukkah. Maybe she would have to throw her centerpiece away, too.

When Rebecca got home, she tried to stop thinking about the decoration. She no longer wanted to talk to Mama about the school project.

"Are you going to feed the pigeons again?" Mama asked. Rebecca nodded. Caring for the pigeons would help take her mind off the centerpiece. Perhaps today she would find out about the mysterious message that had arrived on the white pigeon.

"I've got some chicken soup for Mr. Rossi," Mama said. "It will help his cold. You can take it down when you go to get the bird food."

Mr. Rossi was still his cranky self when he answered his door. "Don't let in the cold air," he scolded, barely opening the door a crack. He had tied a wool scarf around his neck and tucked it into his bathrobe. He quickly took the jar of warm soup and handed out the seed and water pails. "Don't forget to bring me cat's dish, too. She's gonna need lotsa milk."

Rebecca spoke up quickly, before he turned away. "Excuse me," she began. "What message did the white—"

But the old man loudly cleared his throat with a gurgling sound. "Your mama is a nice lady," he said gruffly through the narrow opening. He hesitated as if he was reluctant to say anything pleasant and then added *"Grazie"* as he firmly shut the door.

Rebecca climbed the stairs to the roof. The pairs of pigeons in each cage nestled close to each other for warmth. Some had tucked their heads under their wings, content in their sheltered nook. The white pigeon stood alone on its perch.

What was the secret message Mr. Rossi had received? Maybe Sadie was right that it was about the war in Europe. Only last week, Rebecca had heard Papa worrying out loud that America might end up in the war, too. Could Mr. Rossi be training carrier pigeons for the United States Army? She caught her breath. Imagine such extraordinary goings-on, right here in an ordinary row house!

Rebecca thought about this as she fed the cooing pigeons. If only people could appreciate how her row house was different from all the rest. In her book, Rebecca Randall said it made a big difference what you called things. Instead of plain old Randall Farm, Rebecca called her home Sunnybrook Farm so that people who heard the name would picture the sparkling brook and the sunlit fields. No one would guess her farmhouse looked like any other.

*Perhaps I should give my home a name, too,* Rebecca mused. She looked at the birds and concentrated. She wanted a name that painted a picture of the cozy pigeon roost—and also hinted of hidden secrets.

"I know!" she said out loud. "Pigeon Cove. From now on, I live at Pigeon Cove."

# A Perfect Present

t school on Friday, Rebecca's class helped to decorate the auditorium. The boys climbed on chairs and hung paper snowflakes in the large windows. Rebecca helped the girls drape paper chains made with red and green links along the edge of the stage. A glittering Christmas tree decorated with candles and thin peppermint sticks stood next to the American flag. But Rebecca didn't feel part of the excitement. She was too worried about what to do with the centerpiece she had made. Today was the day she had to take it home.

Back in the classroom, Rebecca's eyes were constantly drawn to the collection of festive centerpieces that covered a huge table against the wall. Each time she looked behind her, the decorations seemed to take up more space, growing like magic evergreens in her imagination.

"As soon as you've put on your coats and hats, you may pick up your decorations," Miss Maloney told the students at the end of the day. "Carry them carefully on your way home."

The room seemed to swirl around Rebecca in a dizzying kaleidoscope of colors as students hurried from the coat closet to the table, pulling on thick woolen mittens and tugging at their trailing scarves. The festive centerpieces were carried out in a parade of ribbons and greenery.

Rebecca's throat felt tight and dry as she lingered at the table. Her centerpiece sat alone, looking abandoned. What should she do with it?

"I hope your family enjoys the gift you made," Miss Maloney said, smiling.

"Thank you," Rebecca said politely, but she was sure the only gifts her family would enjoy were the ones she had made with her sisters.

The sharp air stung Rebecca's cheeks as she stepped outside. Ahead of her, she caught a glimpse of Rose, Gertie, and Lucy as they disappeared across the park.

Rebecca trudged home the long way around. She needed time to think. She had to decide what to do with her decoration before she got back to Pigeon Cove.

As Rebecca passed a row of stores with small heaps of trash piled next to the curb, a flash of red caught her eye. A centerpiece leaned against a stack of old newspapers. There were globs of white glue on some of the branches, and a red candle tilted to one side. It was Rose's decoration. Rebecca couldn't bear to see it tossed out with the trash. She hated the thought of throwing away her own centerpiece. But what choice did she have?

Big flakes of snow began to fall from the thick gray sky. She hurried across the street, dodging a delivery wagon. The horse was draped in a red blanket, and his ears stuck up through slits on each side of a floppy green hat. "Merry Christmas!" called the man driving the wagon. Rebecca gave him a halfhearted wave.

Just before she turned onto her street, she stopped next to a pile of empty wooden crates. Wisps of packing straw littered the sidewalk and blew against the lamppost. Rebecca set her centerpiece down on a broken crate and took one final look at what she had made. The red candle rose above the fresh greens, and she could almost picture a small flame flickering at the top. Just as she bent over to breathe in the woodsy fragrance for the last time, a man came storming out of a shop behind her.

"Get away," he shouted. "Leave that stuff alone!"

Rebecca grabbed her centerpiece and hurried off. The shopkeeper must have thought she was picking through his trash—but she had only been leaving something behind.

The snowflakes fell steadily. By the time Rebecca arrived at her apartment, they had blanketed the sidewalk and covered everything with a layer of white. Rebecca shook off her scarf and unbuttoned her coat before climbing the steps to her apartment. Her stomach fluttered. *Please let Mama be there*, she wished, *and not Bubbie*. She hoped Mama would understand why she had made the decoration and not get angry. She took a deep, raggedy breath and trudged up the stairs.

The mouthwatering smell of frying potato pancakes filled the hallway. Mama was home! Rebecca pushed open the door, but instead of her mother standing at the stove, it was Bubbie who was dropping spoonfuls of lumpy potato batter into the sizzling frying pan.

Quickly, Rebecca hid the centerpiece under her coat.

"Happy Hanukkah," Bubbie cried, lifting a browned potato pancake from the pan and adding it to a pile on a platter. "Come have a little taste. You can *nosh* on a hot latke before everybody comes."

Benny was spinning a dreidel across the table, next to the vegetable grater. Peeled potatoes were heaped in a bowl beside it. "I'm going to win all the candies tonight when we play dreidel," Benny said.

"Where's Mama?" Rebecca gulped.

"Upstairs in my kitchen, having a nice quiet bath," Bubbie replied. "Come, take off your coat, nosh a little, and then grate some more potatoes for me."

Rebecca couldn't take off her coat or Bubbie would see what she was hiding. Quickly, she picked up a potato and tried to grate it with one hand while she held on to the centerpiece with her other hand. The heat in the kitchen felt suffocating.

"What you are doing?" Bubbie scolded. "Take off coat and wash hands first."

"I see a secret!" Benny announced. He started dancing around Rebecca, pointing to the bulge under her coat. "What are you hiding? Is it a surprise?"

Bubbie turned away from the sizzling oil and wiped her hands on her apron. Rebecca felt as if the oil was boiling inside her, sputtering and crackling. She swallowed hard, pushing back the lump in her throat, and pulled out the Christmas decoration.

"I'm s-sorry, Bubbie!" she stammered, tears welling in her eyes. "It was a school project."

Bubbie took the centerpiece from Rebecca and turned it around in her hands. Rebecca couldn't meet her grandmother's eyes. Her head hung down and she rubbed her shoe against a rough nick in the linoleum floor. The only sound she heard was the sizzling of latkes in the frying pan. Bubbie was silent.

Slowly, Rebecca lifted her eyes. But instead of the angry frown she expected, Bubbie's eyes were crinkled at the corners, and she was smiling.

"What's to be sorry?" she said, pinching Rebecca's cheek. "It's a beautiful thing you made." She set it on the table as Benny leaned in for a closer look. The twins came in, dressed in matching wool skirts with crisp white shirtwaists. Bubbie motioned them over. "Come give a look!" she said.

"Oooh," crooned Sophie, "it's so pretty. Did you

make it, Beckie?" Rebecca nodded cautiously.

"I love it," Sadie said. "Especially the little berries."
She brushed them lightly with her fingertips.

"I was going to throw it away on my way home
from school," Rebecca blurted out, "but I just couldn't."
Bubbie and everything around her blurred as tears
spilled down Rebecca's hot cheeks. "I didn't know
what to do. Miss Maloney said all Americans celebrate
Christmas."

Bubbie put her hands on Rebecca's shoulders
and looked into her eyes. "Teacher is right, and she
is wrong," Bubbie said. "Some Americans celebrate
Christmas, and some don't. But at school, you must do
what teacher tells you." She turned to the centerpiece
again. "Now, such a piece of work! What shall we do
with it?"

Rebecca wiped her eyes. "I don't want it, Bubbie.
Let's just throw it away."

"Oh, that would be awful," Sadie said. "Let's leave it
for now, and decide later." Sophie nodded.

Bubbie clapped her hands together. "So, finish grat-
ing potatoes, then feed pigeons, then wash up and put
on clean dress before everyone comes." She turned back

to the latkes, flipping them to brown on the other side.

"We'll take care of the potatoes, Beckie," Sadie offered. "You'll need time to get changed."

"Why bother," Rebecca mumbled. "Who wants to wear a boring old school dress on Hanukkah?"

Bubbie handed Rebecca a jar of vegetable soup. "Is for your Mr. Rossi, his cold should get better."

Rebecca hugged Bubbie tightly. "I thought you would be so angry with me," she whispered.

"For doing a good job with your schoolwork? Never!" Bubbie kissed Rebecca's forehead gently.

Rebecca took the jar of soup and walked slowly down the stairs to Mr. Rossi's door. His window was dark, and she could barely see a faint light coming from the back. She knocked, shivering as snowflakes blew against her face.

Mr. Rossi opened the door just a little wider than usual, grabbed Rebecca's sleeve, and pulled her in. "Quick! Close the door!" he ordered, rubbing his hands together. "It's so cold, and now snow!"

Rebecca shifted from one foot to the other, surprised to find herself inside Mr. Rossi's apartment instead of peering through a crack in the doorway. She wrinkled her nose at an awful smell that filled the air. Something on the stove was steaming and giving off a sour stink. What a difference from the tempting aroma of Bubbie's latkes! She quickly handed Mr. Rossi the soup and edged back to the door.

"I'm feeling better since your mama sends me soup," he said. He pointed to the steaming pot. "The vinegar and salt is helping, too."

Rebecca cringed. "You're drinking vinegar and salt?" *No wonder Mr. Rossi is as sour as an old pickle,* she thought. *He drinks vinegar!*

"Oh, no," Mr. Rossi corrected her. "Not drink it. It's to gargle, for killing the germs."

While he shuffled off in his felt slippers to get the birdseed and a saucer of milk, Rebecca looked around the dim apartment, trying to breathe through her mouth and not her nose. Yellowed doilies were draped over the arms of a sagging couch, and a worn table-cloth covered a small kitchen table. The apartment felt strangely quiet, as if something was missing.

"Don't spill any," Mr. Rossi warned as he handed Rebecca the seed pails. "Even birdseed costs plenty." He reached for the doorknob.

A Perfect Present

If Mr. Rossi was getting better, then this might be her last chance to ask about the secret message. She fidgeted with the fringes on her scarf. She couldn't be shy now. "What was in the message?" she blurted out.

Mr. Rossi covered his mouth with a handkerchief as a new fit of coughing began. For a moment, Rebecca thought she would have to leave again without solving the mystery of the message. But finally Mr. Rossi cleared his throat and said hoarsely, "Is a note from my brother, Aldo, who lives in New Jersey." He swept his arm through the air, as if New Jersey were thousands of miles away instead of just across the Hudson River. "We both keep homing pigeons, just like we did back in Italy. I keep a couple of his birds to send back to him with notes, and he keeps some of mine to fly to me. Pigeons go much faster than mail."

"Was it bad news?" she asked cautiously.

"Ah, no," Mr. Rossi said. "Aldo invites me to come spend Christmas with his family."

Rebecca had never thought about Mr. Rossi having a family somewhere. "I didn't know you had a brother," she said.

"I gotta big family, just like you. Some stay in Italy,

but Aldo, he come to America with me. He gotta lot of children, all grown up, and they all bring their kids to Aldo's for Christmas." Mr. Rossi looked wistful. "I'd love to see the little ones, and Aldo's wife is a good cook. But since they moved to New Jersey, is so far away." Mr. Rossi sighed.

Rebecca would never have guessed that Mr. Rossi would want to spend Christmas with a roomful of children. "It really isn't that far away," she said. "You can take the ferry and be across the river in New Jersey in twenty minutes. Our cousin Max goes there every day to work for a movie company."

Mr. Rossi scratched the gray stubble on his chin and seemed to consider this. "Twenty minutes, you say? If I am feeling better, and you would feed the pigeons and cat while I am gone," he said, almost to himself, "maybe . . ." For the first time, he looked directly at Rebecca, and she saw a glimmer in his eyes. "I write Aldo a note. Can you send it back?"

Rebecca felt a thrill of excitement. "I think I can." She was going to send a message by carrier pigeon! Even Rebecca of Sunnybrook Farm never got to do *that*. She waited until Mr. Rossi handed her a tightly rolled slip of paper. It was so small, she could hardly believe that he had written a message inside. She tucked it into her pocket, took the pails, and headed back outside. Mr. Rossi shuffled behind her.

"Choose one of the gray pigeons," he said hoarsely. "They belong to Aldo, so they know the way." He cupped his hands together. "Hold the bird like this, carry to the edge of the roof, and toss it into the air," he said. "Be careful not to fall!"

"How does the pigeon know where to go?" Rebecca asked in amazement.

"Goes home, always home," Mr. Rossi said.

A snowy hush hung over the rooftop as Rebecca stepped to the cages. She fed one of the gray pigeons first, giving it extra seed. It would need a lot of strength to fly to New Jersey. When all the others were fed, she reached for the bird. Cupping it carefully in her hand, she felt its warmth and the rapid beating of its tiny heart. She tucked the paper message securely into the metal tube on its leg.

Rebecca carried the gray pigeon to the low wall that surrounded the roof. Below her, the East Side was blanketed with white. A few electric lights glowed faintly through apartment windows, and gaslights flickered in others. Soon, Rebecca knew, Jewish families would light the shammas and the first candle in their menorahs. The bright flames would welcome the first night of Hanukkah.

Rebecca held the pigeon close to her face and felt its warm feathers against her cold cheek. "Fly!" she whispered. "Fly home!" She opened her hands, and the bird rose gracefully into the sky.

Rebecca checked on the kittens, watching as they squirmed against their mother. Then she hurried back to her apartment, washed up, and went to change. Her holiday dress looked crisp and bright, but the sight of it filled her with disappointment. How could she have outgrown her best dress before she had worn it more than a few times? She lifted a starched but faded school dress from its hook.

"Aren't you going to wear your New Year's dress?" Sadie asked her.

"It's so pretty on you," Sophie added.

Rebecca felt her face flush. Since her sisters had let her help with the Hanukkah presents, she'd thought they had changed. Now she realized they were going to be as mean as ever. "You know Mama said it's too short," she snapped. "You don't have to make me feel worse."

"Mama could be wrong," Sadie said with a mischievous gleam in her eye. She pushed the dress at Rebecca. "You should try it on. Don't you agree, Sophie?"

"Definitely," her sister said. "I don't think you've grown much at all."

Rebecca fumed. *They still think I'm just a baby!* She wouldn't let them get away with teasing her like this. She tossed the dress onto her bed, but Sadie picked it up again.

"We'll help," Sophie said, pulling off the school dress Rebecca was wearing. Before Rebecca could fend them off, Sadie slipped the holiday dress over Rebecca's head.

"Take it off!" Rebecca protested. "It's too short."

"Not anymore," Sadie said.

Sophie grinned. "We fixed it for you!"

As the dress settled over her shoulders, Rebecca looked down. The cuffs reached the ends of her wrists, and the hem fell just above her knees. She was speechless.

"Happy Hanukkah!" Sadie and Sophie said

together. "Did you think we wouldn't have a gift for you, too?"

Rebecca didn't know what to think. "It's perfect," she murmured.

"I sewed the left sleeve," Sadie said proudly.

"While I sewed the right," Sophie added. "We did the hem together and met in the middle!"

Rebecca looked down at the dress again and then up at her sisters. "Oh, thank you!" she said, throwing her arms around them both. *"Now* it feels like a holiday."* Sophie smoothed the skirt, and Sadie brushed Rebecca's hair to a shine and tied on a festive ribbon. Rebecca beamed.

"I'd better go return Mr. Rossi's pails before he thinks I fell off the roof!" she said.

"He's such an old crab," said Sadie. "No wonder he lives by himself."

That's what was missing from Mr. Rossi's silent, dreary apartment—family! But his life hadn't always been so different from hers, Rebecca realized. He had grown up with a big family, too.

"Maybe he wasn't always so grouchy," Rebecca said. "Maybe he's just lonely." Then she thought of something else. She dashed through the kitchen, stopping only to plant a kiss on her grandmother's cheek. She threw on her shawl, picked up the centerpiece, and bounded down the stairs.

Mr. Rossi opened his door just enough to reach for the pails, but before he could close it again, Rebecca thrust her arm through the opening and handed him the decoration. "Merry Christmas, Mr. Rossi," she said.

Mr. Rossi pulled the door wide open and beckoned her inside. He took the centerpiece and carefully set it on a small table in front of the window. Rebecca thought his eyes looked moist, but perhaps that was from his cold.

"*Bellissimo!*" he said. "You made this?"

Rebecca didn't know what *bellissimo* meant, so she wasn't sure if Mr. Rossi liked the decoration or not. "I-I made it at school," she stammered. "I hope you like it."

Mr. Rossi shuffled over to a chipped cabinet and opened a drawer at the very bottom. "You're a good girl to take care of birds while I was sick," he said. "And you found my little Pasta, with her new family. Not many kids around here would do favors for me." He took a cloth bundle from the drawer and carefully unrolled two sparkling blue glass candlesticks. He handed them to Rebecca.

"I know you don't celebrate Christmas," he said. "But you light candles for Hanukkah. These belonged to my wife, a long time ago. I want for you to have them. You can light candles and enjoy them as she did, yes?"

"Oh, Mr. Rossi," Rebecca gasped, "they're beautiful." She looked at the old man and thought she saw a wisp of a smile. "Grazie," she said.

Rebecca stepped outside and closed the door with a soft click. Snow capped the graceful arches of the streetlamps and coated the stoop and the carved lion heads over the doorway. Even under the blanket of snow, she could still recognize the distinctive shape of each familiar thing in her neighborhood.

Rebecca turned to see Mr. Rossi lighting the tall red candle in the centerpiece. The window was bathed in its flickering glow. Mr. Rossi could enjoy his Christmas decoration from inside, and Rebecca could enjoy it from the outside.

Rebecca realized that Mr. Rossi wasn't at all the person she had thought he was. Now that she knew more about him, Mr. Rossi seemed rather special. After all, how many people could turn an ordinary row house into a pigeon cove?

Rebecca held the glass candlesticks close and smiled. They might not be right for Hanukkah, as Mr. Rossi thought, but they were perfect for the Sabbath.

Close by, Rebecca heard the sound of laughing and singing. She was sure she heard cousin Max's voice booming out a song through the night. "Hanukkah, oh Hanukkah, come light the menorah . . ."

Uncle Jacob and Aunt Fannie came around the corner, carrying platters of food. Cousin Max was holding a big seltzer bottle and singing at the top of his lungs. Ana and her brothers were skipping and skidding through the slippery snow that covered the sidewalk.

"Happy Hanukkah!" Rebecca called gaily. "Welcome to Pigeon Cove!"

# INSIDE Rebecca's World

When Rebecca was growing up, thousands of immigrants were coming to America each year to make new lives. Cities often had entire neighborhoods settled by people from one country. Most immigrants entered the U.S. at New York City's Ellis Island, as Ana's family did. The largest city in America, New York, had millions of Jewish immigrants from Russia and other countries.

In 1914, the Russian empire was ruled by the powerful tsar. The tsar did not regard his Jewish subjects as real Russians, because the Jews practiced a different religion and spoke a different language: Yiddish. Jews were barred from most jobs and could not own land or travel freely. Even worse, Russian soldiers and villagers sometimes led *pogroms*, or violent attacks on Jews. They broke into Jewish homes, shops, and temples, looting and burning—and often killing, too. They did this out of *prejudice*, the belief that people who are different are bad.

Jews like Rebecca's and Ana's parents decided to move to countries where their families could lead better lives. Between 1880 and 1914, two million Jews left Russia and Eastern Europe and came to the United States.

Immigrants brought the traditions of their old countries to America, but they adapted to new ways, too. Most of the Jewish immigrants spoke Yiddish, like Rebecca's grandparents, but they learned English. On Friday evenings, Jewish families welcomed the Sabbath with candles and prayers. The Sabbath, which lasted until sundown on Saturday, was supposed to be a day of rest, but like Rebecca's papa, many Jews had to work on Saturday to feed their families. The immigrants who followed Jewish traditions more strictly, like Bubbie and Grandpa, often disapproved of those who did not. This conflict between old ways and new ways is one that all immigrants face when they move to a new country.

Whether they had been in America for generations or were newcomers, most Americans enjoyed attending vaudeville shows, which had a variety of song and dance acts, comedians, magicians, and even animal acts. Many movie actors got their start in vaudeville, just like cousin Max did. By 1914, vaudeville theaters were also showing movies. Especially popular were serials, such as *The Perils of Pauline,* which showed a new episode every week.

Before the main feature, theaters would show a *newsreel,* a short film about current events. People were eager to see newsreels about the First World War, which had just broken out in Europe. Although the U.S. had not yet entered the war, Americans were keenly interested in it. Jews were especially concerned about their relatives back in Russia and raised millions of dollars to help them.

After the war started, it became much more difficult to leave Europe. In contrast to the millions of immigrants who had come in the previous years, only a few more people were able to get out of Russia, as Ana's family did, and come to safety in America.

# GLOSSARY

**Amerikanka** (ah-mair-ee-KONG-kah)—the Russian way to say *American*

**Bar Mitzvah** (bar MITS-vah)—the ceremony honoring a boy's first reading of the Hebrew Bible before the congregation, and also the boy himself. Hebrew for "son of the commandment."

**bellissimo** (bel-LEES-see-moh)—Italian for *very beautiful*

**bubbie** (BUH-bee)—the Yiddish word for *grandmother*

**chutzpah** (HOOTS-pah; first syllable rhymes with "puts")—the Yiddish way of saying *boldness, nerve*

**dreidel** (DRAY-dl)—in Yiddish, a toy marked with Hebrew letters and spun like a top; also, the game played with a dreidel

**gelt** (gelt)—a Yiddish word for *money*

**grazie** (GRAHT-see-eh)—the Italian word for *thank you*

**hallah** (HAH-lah; often spelled "challah")—a Hebrew word for a rich white bread made with eggs and usually braided

**Hanukkah** (HAH-nik-ah)—a holiday to honor the Jews' victory in regaining their temple in Jerusalem; Hebrew for "dedication"

**knish** (kuh-NISH)—in Yiddish, a food made of dough stuffed with a filling, such as potato, then baked or fried

**kopek** (KOH-pek)—a small *Russian coin*, similar to a penny

**kugel** (KOO-gl; first syllable rhymes with "good")—in Yiddish, a baked casserole usually made with noodles or potatoes

**latke** (LOT-keh)—the Yiddish word for a *potato pancake*

**mazel tov** (MAH-zl tof)—Hebrew for *congratulations!*

**menorah** (men-OR-ah)—a Hebrew word for *candelabra*

**mitzvah** (MITS-vah)—a good deed, and also the duty to perform acts of kindness. Hebrew for "commandment."

**nosh** (nosh)—*to snack*, in Yiddish

**nudge** (nooj; same vowel sound as in "wood")—in Yiddish, a pushy *pest*

**oy vey** (oy VAY)—a Yiddish exclamation meaning *"oh dear!"*

**pushke** (PUSH-kee)—in Yiddish, a small can or box used to collect money for charity

**rugalach** (ROO-gul-ahk)—a Yiddish word meaning "little twists"; a small pastry, often filled with nuts or jam

**samovar** (SAM-oh-var)—a *Russian urn* used to heat water for tea

**schlepping** (SHLEP-ing)—a Yiddish word that means *hauling* or *lugging*

**scusi** (SKOO-zee)—*Excuse me* in Italian

**Shabbos** (SHAH-bes)—Yiddish for *Sabbath*, the day of rest

**shah** (shah)—the Yiddish way to say *shush!*

**shammas** (SHAH-mes)—the ninth candle on the Hanukkah menorah that is used to light all the others; from a Hebrew word meaning "servant"

**trousseau** (troo-SOH)—the household goods that a bride brings to her marriage. Originally a French word.

**tsar** (zar; often spelled "czar")—the Russian word for *emperor*

**yarmulke** (YAH-muh-kah)—in Yiddish, a *skullcap* worn by Jewish men to show respect for God

**zayda** (ZAY-dah)—*grandfather* in Yiddish

# Read more of REBECCA'S stories,

available from booksellers and at *americangirl.com*

## ⨀ *Classics* ⨀

*Rebecca's classic series, now in two volumes:*

*Volume 1:*

**The Sound of Applause**

Rebecca uses her talents to help cousin Ana escape Russia. Now she must share everything with Ana—even the stage!

*Volume 2:*

**Lights, Camera, Rebecca!**

Rebecca gets the best birthday present ever—a role in a real movie. But she can't tell anyone in her family about it.

## ⨀ *Journey in Time* ⨀

*Travel back in time—and spend a day with Rebecca!*

### The Glow of the Spotlight

Step inside Rebecca's world and the excitement of New York City in 1914! Bargain with street peddlers, and audition for a Broadway show. Choose your own path through this multiple-ending story.

## ⨀ *Mysteries* ⨀

*More thrilling adventures with Rebecca!*

### The Crystal Ball

Will a visit to a fortune teller reveal the truth about Mr. Rossi?

### A Bundle of Trouble

Rebecca realizes the baby she's caring for is in danger—and so is she.

### Secrets at Camp Nokomis

Rebecca's camp bunkmate seems nice, but what is she hiding?

*⌒⌒ A Sneak Peek at ⌒⌒*

# Lights, Camera, Rebecca!

*A Rebecca Classic*

*Volume 2*

Rebecca's adventures continue in the
second volume of her classic stories.

ho's the doll-baby in the scrumptious hat?" said a sweet voice. An actress was walking up the hallway, carrying a brown wig with flowing ringlets.

"This is my cousin, Rebecca Rubin," Max said. "Rebecca, meet Miss Lillian Armstrong."

Rebecca smiled shyly and found she could barely speak. "Glad to meet you," she managed.

"Say, how would you like to see me turn from a real girl into a movie actress?" Miss Armstrong asked. Rebecca nodded, unable to say a word.

Miss Armstrong opened her dressing room door. Painted on the outside was a shiny gold star with her name in black lettering just underneath. Rebecca wondered if Max had a star painted on his door, too. Inside the small room, the wallpaper was printed with white lilies, and a vase of fresh lilies perched on the corner of the dressing table.

"First of all, you must call me Lily," said the actress. "We aren't very formal here." She pointed to an upholstered chaise longue. "Make yourself comfortable." Lily placed the wig on top of a coat tree and kicked off her shoes. She stepped behind a Chinese folding screen and tossed her clothes across the top. A moment later, she emerged wearing a long flowered robe and settled gracefully on a stool at her dressing table. She opened a small case and lined up a row of jars and foil-covered sticks.

"Why do you have to wear all that makeup?" Rebecca asked politely.

"Without it, my face would photograph as a dark shadow. And after I make my skin pale, I've got to darken around my eyes, or they wouldn't show up at all. I know I look odd," Lily admitted, "but it all comes out bright and natural on film."

A light knock sounded on the door. *"Entrez!"* Lily called. A plump woman came in with an evening gown draped over her arm.

"My dress!" Lily exclaimed. She dropped her dressing robe on the floor and held her arms straight up in the air. Mabel pulled the dress over the actress's head. It swished down around Lily's dainty ankles, and Mabel began looping tiny buttons up the back. Lily strapped on a pair of delicate shoes that were more elegant than any in Papa's shoe store. Mabel picked up the clothes Lily had left strewn about. She clucked her disapproval, just as Bubbie would, but Lily didn't seem to notice.

"Shall we?" Lily asked, offering her arm to Rebecca. Together they walked toward the set.

"What happens in the movie?" Rebecca asked.

"Well, my parents have chosen a rich man for me to marry, but I don't like him. I would rather die than marry such a cad!" She changed her expression to a dreamy look and sighed deeply. "I'm secretly in love with the gardener. Of course, my parents wouldn't ever approve, and there's the plot."

Rebecca thought the story sounded a lot like real life. In fact, it sounded a bit like her own life. *Only in my case,* she realized, *it's movies I'm in love with—and my parents would never approve!*

Lily pushed open heavy double doors, and Rebecca entered a huge room with a glass ceiling. Light flooded across a stone patio with a carved railing and two stately urns overflowing with paper flowers. Behind the patio, the front of a mansion was painted on a large canvas backdrop. The mansion looked so real, Rebecca almost believed she could step inside. But the workings of the movie studio intruded into the illusion with wires, cameras, and rows of spotlights.

Don Herringbone entered the studio, his face

covered with pasty makeup and his eyebrows darkened, giving him a menacing look.

"There's my wicked suitor," Lily laughed.

"Lillian, my dear," he said. He took her hand and
lightly kissed it. "You know you're in love with me!"
Lily drew back coyly, her head turned to one side.

Rebecca was fascinated. Was this part of their act?

Just then, Max walked over. He wore rough pants
with suspenders buttoned over a loose white shirt,
open at the neck. His hair fell in tousled waves under
a soft cap.

"Ah, the gardener," Mr. Herringbone drawled,
sounding haughty.

"Beware this scoundrel in fancy clothes," Max advised Lily.

Rebecca felt a shiver of delight. Were they all acting? Why, acting for a movie didn't seem any different from pretending with her friends. Rebecca could
playact, too. She gestured toward Lily with a flick of
her hand and spoke in a high voice. "I'm sure such an
elegant lady knows her best suitor."

"You bet I do, doll-baby," Lily laughed.

Max coughed a little. "Come on, Rebecca," he said,

steering her away from the group. "Let's find you a good spot to watch from."

At one side of the room, the actresses and actors who had been on the ferry leaned against walls, sat on chairs, and perched on props. "Welcome to the garden," said an actress in a feathered hat. "In case you can't tell, we're all lowly worms, just waiting to be dug up. Extras like us just wriggle around, hoping the Grand Pooh-Bah will pick us for a scene—any scene, just so we can pay the rent! Otherwise, it's move back in with Mama." The other extras groaned.

Another young actress glared at Rebecca. Her lips were painted fire-engine red and her glossy nails were long and tapered. "Are you competition, or just visiting?"

"I'm just here to watch," Rebecca assured her. "I'm not an actress."

"Bet you'd like to be, though," the actress replied.

Rebecca squirmed under her steady gaze. How had she guessed what Rebecca was thinking? The actress turned to the other extras. "Watch out for this one," she warned, pointing a long-nailed finger at Rebecca.

# About the Author

JACQUELINE DEMBAR GREENE used
to read historical novels under an apple tree
in her yard when she was a girl. She loved to
imagine living in a more exciting time and
place. While writing about Rebecca, Ms.
Greene talked with friends and relatives who
recalled their experiences growing up in the
early 1900s. She also explored New York's
Lower East Side and visited the neighborhoods that would have been part of Rebecca's
world. Ms. Greene lives in Massachusetts
with her husband. When she isn't writing,
she enjoys hiking, gardening, and traveling
to visit her two grown sons.